D1506951

Usborne

Illustrated
Classics

Huckleberry Finn
and other stories

Usborne Illustrated Classics

Huckleberry Finn
and other stories

Contents

The Adventures of Huckleberry Finn   7
Based on a story by Mark Twain
Adapted by Rob Lloyd Jones
Illustrated by Andy Elkerton

The Strange Case of Dr. Jekyll and Mr. Hyde   69
Based on a story by Robert Louis Stevenson
Adapted by Rob Lloyd Jones
Illustrated by Victor Tavares

Kidnapped   131
Based on a story by Robert Louis Stevenson
Adapted by Rob Lloyd Jones
Illustrated by Alan Marks

King Solomon's Mines 193
Based on a story by H. Rider Haggard
Adapted by Russell Punter
Illustrated by Matteo Pincelli

White Fang 255
Based on a story by Jack London
Adapted by Sarah Courtauld
Illustrated by Alan Marks

The Phantom of the Opera 317
Based on a story by Gaston Leroux
Adapted by Kate Knighton
Illustrated by Victor Tavares

About the Authors 378

The Adventures of

Huckleberry Finn

This story is set in the southern states of America in the 1880s, when rich white landowners used slaves — black men and women forced to work for them by law. These people were bought and sold like animals, and had no rights of their own.

Chapter 1

Me and Tom Sawyer

This book is all about me, Huckleberry Finn, and here's something you should know straight off: I'm only happy when I'm wearing rags.

I used to wear nothing but rags, when I lived in a barrel in St. Petersburg, on the shore of the mighty Mississippi River. But for some reason no one wanted me to sleep in a barrel. A fussy, wrinkled old woman named Widow Douglas made me live in her home with her sister Miss Watson, who was even more fussy and much more wrinkled.

They hugged me so hard I could barely breathe, and they wept over me and called me a poor lost little orphan.

I don't know why they said that – I wasn't really an orphan. I had a dad, Pap, but he was a real mean old beggar and he beat me terribly.

That was when I ran away to live in a barrel.

Widow Douglas had a big old house, where everything was just spick and span. I never saw one speck of dust anywhere among its gloomy halls. She gave me new clothes, but I found them itchy and felt all cramped up.

They rang a bell for supper, and Miss Watson always said prayers before we ate. I did too, even though I never saw much point in praying. Nothing ever came of it, and I told them so.

"Don't talk such nonsense, Huckleberry!" Widow Douglas snapped. "And don't put your feet on the furniture!"

"Sit up straight please!" Miss Watson barked. "Do try to behave!"

It was torture!

One night, I sat staring out of my bedroom window, watching the willow branches sway by the river. I felt as if the wind was calling me back to my old life…

Just then, I saw someone hiding among the trees.

Psst, the person hissed.

My heart jumped for joy. It was my old pal Tom Sawyer! Tom and I had been on adventures together before I moved in with Widow Douglas. And I could tell from the grin on his face that he was looking for another.

"I'm forming a gang of robbers," Tom declared. "Do you want to join?"

He didn't need to ask twice. Quickly, I scrambled through the window, pulled it shut and dropped to the ground.

We crept across the garden, through stripes of moonlight and shadow. Miss Watson owned several slaves, and one of them, Jim, was sitting against a tree, smoking a pipe. We sneaked past him, and darted into the woods.

Tom's younger brother, Sid, was waiting, and we charged through the forest, hooting and hollering. We chased wild hogs, and fought like pirates with sticks. I felt alive and free again, just like in the good old days.

By the time I got back to the house, I was covered
in mud and exhausted, but also grinning from ear
to ear.

The smile slipped from my face as I saw that my
bedroom window was open. I was sure I had shut it
as I sneaked out.

Cautiously, I climbed through. My hand trembled
as I lit a candle, and the light skittered
around the bedroom walls.

There, in the shadows,
was my father!

Chapter 2
Pap

Pap stepped from the gloom. His clothes were rags, and filthy toes poked from the ends of his battered boots. A straggly, greasy beard hung from his flushed face. He looked like an ogre with his staring eyes, which were dark and fierce and glinted in the candlelight.

"Look at you," Pap growled. "Dressed up all nice and tidy."

I wasn't scared. Pap was just a bully. But he was stronger than me, so I had to be careful.

"I need some money," he demanded.

"I'm not giving you anything," I said.

"We'll see about that!"

He grabbed me and dragged me from the house. I thrashed and kicked, but his grip only tightened on my arm. He hurled me into a canoe by the river, and paddled to the opposite shore, where thick woodland rose from the riverbank.

Pap locked me up in a log cabin, and that's where I stayed for several weeks. There seemed no hope of escape – the cabin window was barred and too small to squeeze through, the chimney was too narrow to climb up, and the door was a foot-thick slab of wood.

During the day, Pap went out hunting with a shotgun. At night, he moaned and grumbled about his hard life. He beat me a lot too. Most nights I fell asleep covered in bruises.

Then, one day, Pap made a mistake...

He left a rusty old saw in the cabin...

As soon as he went out, I grabbed the tool and started sawing at the log wall. I worked until blisters burst on my hands, and I'd cut a hole big enough to squirm through.

It was dark by the time I escaped. I stumbled through the woods, tripping over, cursing and staggering up. Reaching the riverbank, I clambered into Pap's canoe and pushed it out across the water.

I lay on the bottom of the canoe, my heart hammering so loud I feared Pap might hear it in the woods. I was certain he would cry out, or fire his shotgun. But instead everything fell silent, as the current whisked me along the dark and swirling river.

Chapter 3
Jackson's Island

I lay on the bottom of the canoe, staring up at the moon and the shivering stars. Lumps of driftwood thumped the sides of the boat, but otherwise the night was eerily still.

When I finally dared to look up, I saw the dark, humped shape of Jackson's Island rising in the middle of the wide river. Willow trees leaned from the shore, dipping their spindly branches into the water.

Grabbing a branch, I used it to pull the canoe to the shore and then I collapsed onto the riverbank. I was so exhausted that I just lay down to sleep right there in the long, wet grass.

When I woke, the sun was high above me,
dazzling my eyes. A cool breeze rustled the long
grass. I struggled up and walked further into the
island, among the dark, dense woodland.

Each time the branches creaked, I whirled around
in fright. I was terrified that Pap would find me.

I kept stopping and listening. But all that I could

hear was the wind whispering among the branches, and the frantic hammering of my heart.

Then, ahead, I saw smoke.

I crept closer and crouched behind a bush. A man lay beside a crackling fire, wrapped up in an old horse blanket.

Was it Pap?

As the man sat up, a shaft of sunlight caught his face. It was Jim – Miss Watson's slave! I was so relieved that I burst from the bushes and shouted, "Hello Jim!"

Jim sprang up, his eyes wild with fright. Then he dropped to his knees and slapped his hands together like he was praying. "Oh, please don't tell on me!" he cried.

Once Jim had calmed down, we sat beside the fire and he told me his story.

"I ran off, Huck," he said. "Miss Watson was going to sell me to slave traders in New Orleans. If she did, I'd never see my family again. So I sneaked away and paddled across the river holding onto a log. I've been hiding on this island ever since."

Poor Jim was as thin as a stick. All he'd eaten for days were wild strawberries. So the first thing I did was take his fishing line and catch some catfish in the river. We cooked them over the fire and ate and ate. Then, with our bellies full, we sat together by the flames.

"You promise you won't tell on me, Huck?" Jim said, his voice trembling.

I felt guilty. It was against the law to help runaway slaves. But I promised, and so that was that.

Besides, there was no way I was going back to Miss Watson and Widow Douglas. Now, Jim and I were runaways together.

Chapter 4
On the river

I've never seen such a storm as the one that woke us the next day. Thunder roared and lightning lit the woods. Rain ripped leaves from the trees, and the wind was so strong we could barely walk five paces before it slapped us back to the ground.

The river rose, flooding Jackson's Island.
Splashing through the water, Jim and I made it to
the canoe, and set off along the river.

Water snakes and turtles swam beside the boat.
Then, as we passed the end of the island, I was
amazed to see a small timber house float past.
It must have been washed from the bank by the
floods, and now it was just bobbing around in the
frothing water.

We paddled to it, and climbed in through a window. It was dark inside. As my eyes adjusted to the gloom, I saw an old clothes chest against the wall. And there, beside the chest, lay the body of a man.

"He's dead!" Jim said.

The man had been shot in the back.

"Stay back Huck. Don't look at his face, it's too awful."

Quickly, Jim threw some old rags over the body, hiding the man's face.

I didn't want to see anyway. Instead, I swiped a battered straw hat from the chest. It was a perfect fit. We took some supplies too – an old tin lantern, blankets, and some money from the dead man's pocket. All in all, it was a good haul.

Back in the canoe, I asked Jim about the dead man. But he was scared that the man's ghost might haunt us if we spoke about him, bringing us bad luck, so I didn't ask any more. We were going to need all the good luck we could get.

We kept paddling along the river until an old raft made of pine planks came drifting past.

It looked much more comfortable than our cramped old canoe, so we climbed on board and set the canoe adrift.

We had a plan now, too. In some parts of the country, slavery was banned and Jim would be free.

But it would be a difficult journey. People hunted
runaway slaves for rewards, so it wasn't safe to travel
during the day. Instead, we hid on the riverbanks
and set off again after sunset.

Jim built a little tent on the raft, to keep us dry
in the rain. We caught catfish, swam and lay on our
backs looking up at the stars.

Sometimes we had the whole river to ourselves. Then a huge steamboat would puff past, sparks spurting from its funnels and raining over the river like fireworks.

I tell you, there's no place like a raft.

Everywhere else is cramped by comparison. But on a raft, life is free and easy. All in all I was living pretty well.

To be truthful, Jim wasn't as happy as me.

Sometimes he sat with his head between his knees. Other nights, he didn't even say a word. I knew he was thinking about his wife and children back in St. Petersburg, and wishing he could be with them again.

"You're the only friend I have Huck," he said with a moan. "But as soon as I get my freedom I'm going to save some money and buy my family out of slavery."

Chapter 5

Royal strangers

One morning, as Jim and I were resting by some cottonwood thickets, strange sounds rang along the riverbank. At first we heard snarls and barks, coming closer. Then there were awful loud screams and shouts and calls for help.

Two men raced along the bank. They were being chased by dogs.

"Save our lives!" one of them shrieked.

"We're innocent men!" the other wailed.

They jumped on board the raft, and we pushed off
onto the river. One of the men was bald, with wispy
white whiskers and dark, beady eyes like a shark.
The other was younger, although his face looked as
worn out as the battered old carpet bag he carried.

I asked them what happened and they groaned.

"We were run out of town!" one of the men
exclaimed. "Us!"

"Who are you?" Jim asked.

I saw one of the men throw the other a quick, sly
glance. "Well, I suppose we can tell you," he said.
"I am a duke."

"And I am a king," the other announced. "The
King of France."

Jim stared at them, his mouth open in amazement, but I knew that the men were lying. They were con men, people who tricked others out of their money. That was why they were run out of the town. But I couldn't say anything – after all, Jim and I were runaways too.

That night, I stood with Jim at one end of the raft, wishing we'd never helped them. The King and the Duke kept whispering to each other and chuckling. I knew they were plotting a new trick to swindle money out of people.

Suddenly the Duke bolted up. "We shall stage a show!" he declared.

Both men began prancing around the raft, quoting lines from the plays of William Shakespeare, and acting out elaborate sword fights with sticks.

"Our play will be a certain hit!" the King proclaimed.

I grew more and more worried. What were these rascals planning?

By the time we approached the state of Arkansas, they were ready to perform their play.

We docked the raft near a small town. It was too dangerous for Jim to come with us; someone might turn him in for a reward. So he stayed on the bank, hiding among a grove of cypress trees.

The King and Duke were lucky – there was a small circus camped in the town, so the place was busy. The Duke rented a stage in the courthouse, and the King had some posters printed. We pinned them up all over town.

FOR ONE NIGHT ONLY!

WILLIAM SHAKESPEARE'S THRILLING SWORD FIGHTS, SPEECHES AND LOVE SCENES!

That night, the courthouse was so full that we had to turn people away. As the Duke collected people's money at the door, a sly grin rose across his wrinkled face. He leaned close to me and whispered, "Get ready to run, Huck. Run as if dogs were after you."

The curtain rose and the King burst onto the
stage dressed in the strangest costume I'd ever seen.
He was painted like a rainbow, all over his almost
naked body. For several minutes he skipped around
the stage, reciting lines from Shakespeare's plays.

Then, very suddenly, he ran off – and the stage
curtain fell.

It took the crowd a few minutes to realize they had been swindled.

"Is that all there is?" one of them yelled. "Give us our money back!"

"They're just crooks!" someone else shouted.

By then we were already running as fast as we could to the riverbank. We leaped onto the raft, and Jim shoved it out onto the water.

The King and the Duke shook hands and slapped each other on the back. They laughed until their throats ran dry, and then counted their money from the night.

I watched them with a sigh so heavy it seemed to push the raft faster along the river. I realized that I was now very far from home.

Chapter 6
Betrayed

We had rafted a long way south, and the weather grew warmer. Clumps of feathery moss, like long beards, hung from the trees. At night, fireflies glimmered around us, as if we were floating through stars.

For most of the time, the Duke and King sat together, whispering and muttering. They were looking for a new scam, and soon enough they found one.

At the next village, they pretended to be the long-lost brothers of a dead man, to swindle his poor daughters out of their fortune. But they were chased out of town when the man's real brothers showed up.

After that they just lay around on the raft, cursing everyone in the village.

One night, Jim slid over to me on the raft, and scowled. "They're cheats and frauds, Huck," he said, his voice low. "What are we going to do?"

"I know Jim," I replied. "We've got to give them the slip."

Early the next morning, we stopped at a little village called Pikesville. By then, the Duke and King had both cheered up, which I thought must be bad news. Surely they were planning another scam.

"I will go into the village alone," the King announced. "I'll see if the villagers have heard yet about our tricks, or if they're still able to be swindled. If I am not back by midday, Duke, you must come and find me."

Well, *that* was a long morning. The Duke was restless and grumpy, and snapped at me over everything I said or did.

When midday came, it was a relief to get off the raft. I couldn't see Jim but, guessing he was hiding on the riverbank, I followed the Duke and set off in search of the King.

We finally found him hunched over a drink in the village's dusty tavern, ignoring everyone. He looked as if he'd been there all morning, spending the money from his scams.

Of course the Duke was furious, and began to yell curses at the King. The King yelled the curses right back, and suddenly the two of them were fighting, clattering into tables and then wrestling on the floor.

I seized my chance – and fled. I ran like crazy for the river, yelling to Jim as I got close. "Set the raft loose, Jim. We're leaving them here."

There was no answer.

The raft was empty – Jim was gone!

I called louder, and then yelled at the top of my voice, praying he was hiding among the bushes. My heart pounded against my rib cage. I was desperate with fear for my friend. Where *was* he?

I spotted a boy on the road to the village, and
rushed over to him. "Have you seen a slave around
here?" I asked breathlessly.

A gap-toothed grin spread across the boy's rosy
cheeks. "He's locked up at Silas Phelps's farm," he
replied. "He's a runaway slave." His eyes narrowed.
"Hey, you haven't been helping him, have you?"

There was no point in getting myself into trouble too. If I did, I wouldn't be able to help Jim. "No," I lied. "I, um, I wanted to claim the reward for catching him."

"Well you're too late," the boy said. "An old man in the village turned him in for forty dollars. He's been in the tavern ever since, spending his reward."

I wanted to scream with rage. The boy meant the King – that old swindler was behind this. After all the help we had given him, he'd sold Jim right back into slavery.

I walked back to the raft in a daze. I thought of all the adventures Jim and I had had together. Then I pictured him locked in chains and working again as a slave…

I had to save him.

So I started thinking up a plan.

Chapter 7

Rescue plan

Everything was silent and still when I crept to the Phelps's farm, where I'd been told Jim was being kept in chains. The only sound was the flies, buzzing in the air.

The farm had a big log house for the family, and small wooden cabins for the slaves. I could see slaves working in the cotton fields, struggling under the weight of the loaded baskets on their backs.

But I couldn't see Jim. I wanted to cry out
for him, but couldn't risk being caught.

I jumped the fence and darted for the house, my
heart pounding as fast as my feet. Then... Disaster!

A pack of dogs charged from the house. They
surrounded me, howling and snarling and showing
their vicious teeth. I thought they might eat me
for lunch, but now the farmer's wife ran from the
kitchen, yelling at the beasts. She whacked one
of them on the nose with a rolling pin,
and they all scampered off.

I feared I was caught, but the woman's face lit up with a smile. "It's you!" she cried.

I had no idea who she thought I was, but I nodded and smiled back.

Tears of joy ran down the woman's cheeks, and she grabbed me in a tight hug. "We expected you two days ago, Tom," she said. "Was your boat delayed?"

Cold sweat slid down my back. Who was Tom?

"Yes ma'am," I said hesitantly.

"Oh, call me Aunt Sally! Look Tom, here comes your Uncle Silas."

The farmer stepped from the house; a man with a face as wrinkled as a walnut. "Who's this?" he asked, squinting.

"Why it's Tom Sawyer!" declared Aunt Sally.

My legs turned to jelly and I almost collapsed to the floor. This was my friend Tom Sawyer's aunt and uncle. What luck! I knew enough about Tom's life to pretend to be him, while I searched the farm for Jim.

Then I heard a steamboat whistle from the river, and panic shot up my spine. What if the real Tom Sawyer was on that boat? I had to get to him first, and warn him about what was going on.

Pretending I'd left my bag at the river, I rushed off. As I raced along the road, a boy approached from the other direction. Sure enough – it was Tom.

He stared at me for a long moment, and then we both burst out laughing. We sat by the roadside and I told him all about my adventures, and how Jim was in trouble.

Tom thought about it for a minute, and then sprang up. "Let's say I'm Sid," he said.

Sid was Tom's younger brother. It was a clever plan, since Aunt Sally didn't seem to know what any of the Sawyer family looked like.

As we walked back to the farm, Tom told me all the news from home. I was sad to hear that Miss Watson had died a few weeks back. Pap was gone too, although no one knew where. He'd disappeared around the same time that I ran off with Jim.

We stopped walking as a crowd came marching from the village. They were making all sorts of noise – singing, cheering and banging tin pans, loud enough to drive away the Devil. They seemed delighted about something and, as they came closer, I saw what. They had two prisoners tied to rails – the King and the Duke.

The con men were splattered with sticky black tar and covered with feathers. They must have been caught trying to trick the villagers with one of their scams. I knew that they deserved their punishment but, still, I couldn't help feeling sorry for them. That was a cruel fate for anyone.

Now, though, I had to worry about Jim...

Chapter 8

Break out

Tom's plan worked perfectly. Aunt Sally and Uncle Silas believed that he was Sid, and they were delighted. They hugged him so tight he could barely breathe, and then fed us a huge supper of meatloaf and potatoes.

Throughout the meal, Tom and I kept our eyes peeled for Jim. Then, as we ate, Tom nudged me. We watched a slave carry a plate of food to one of the cabins. The cabin was padlocked and the slave slid the plate under the door.

"There's someone locked up in that cabin," Tom whispered to me.

"I reckon it's Jim," I replied.

Tom sighed, disappointed. "Breaking him out of there will be too easy," he muttered.

"What do you mean?"

"A good escape story should be harder," Tom

explained. "There should be rope ladders and guards, like in adventure stories."

"I'd rather it wasn't hard, Tom. Why don't we just dig under the door?"

"I suppose that will have to do..."

That night, as soon as Aunt Sally and Uncle Silas were asleep, I sneaked outside and stole two shovels from the shed. Tom was waiting for me at the cabins, with a grin on his face and a sack slung over his shoulder.

"What's that for?" I asked.

"You'll see..."

His eyes sparkled with excitement. He was having fun, but I was just scared.

We got to work, digging under the cabin door.

By the time the hole was big enough to scramble under, our arms ached and our hands were covered in blisters.

It was a struggle to squeeze through, and very dark inside the dingy cabin. The air was musty and stank of stale sweat. "Jim?" I whispered.

The voice that came back was parched and trembling. "H...Huck?"

And there he was, cowering on a broken wooden bed. Jim must have been terrified, but he still managed a smile. "Huck!" he said.

"We're breaking you out, Jim!"

"First you need a disguise," Tom said.

He rustled in his sack and pulled out one of Aunt Sally's nightgowns. "In adventure books, prisoners always wear ladies' clothes to escape."

We didn't argue with Tom; we were just grateful for his help. But he sure had a funny way of doing things.

Jim pulled on the disguise, and we helped him crawl to freedom under the door. Suddenly, lights came on in the Phelps's house.

"Who's there?" a voice bellowed.

It was Uncle Silas – and he had a shotgun.

"Run!" I cried.

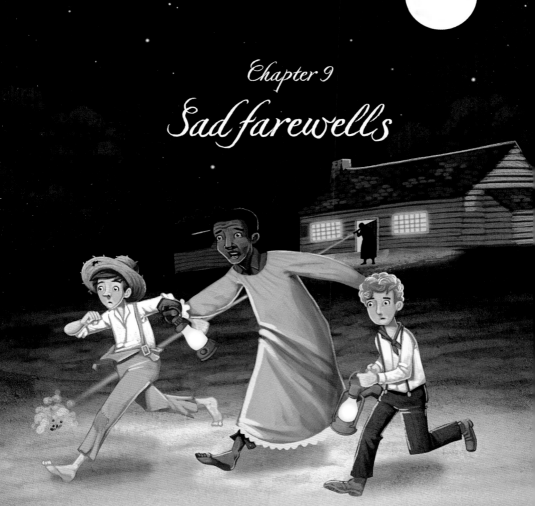

Chapter 9
Sad farewells

Gunshots boomed through the night, frightening crows from the trees. Bullets whizzed past us as we fled the farm and raced for the river.

By the time we reached the raft, we were laughing between gulping, gasping breaths.

"We did it!" I said.

Tom was the happiest of us all – he had a bullet wound in his leg.

I was horrified when I saw the injury. "We have to find a doctor," I said.

"It's only a scratch," Tom insisted. "And now I have a bullet scar, just like the heroes in my books."

"We'd better go, Huck," Jim said, pulling me towards the raft. "The villagers will come hunting for me soon enough."

"Oh don't worry about that," Tom said. "You're a free man, Jim."

Jim looked as confused as I did, but Tom just grinned again. "When Miss Watson died," he explained, "she granted Jim his freedom in her will."

"What?" I cried. "Do you mean that Jim could have been free this whole time? Why didn't you say so earlier?"

"Because it was an adventure!" Tom said.

Like I said, Tom Sawyer had a funny way of doing things.

Jim wasn't angry. In fact, he was so happy that tears streamed down his cheeks.

He hugged me, and then Tom, and then both of us at the same time. "Now I can go back to my family," he said. "What about you, Huck? Will you come back?"

"I can't," I said. "Pap will lock me up again."

The smile fell from Jim's face. When he spoke again, his voice was sad and serious.

"Huck, do you remember that dead man we saw in the floating house?"

I shuddered at the memory. "What about him?"

"That was your Pap, Huck. I'm sorry..."

It was dark news, but I refused to let it upset me. Pap was a no-good bully. He wasn't worth my tears. Secretly, though, my heart ached. I wished things had been different between him and me.

I still didn't go back to St. Petersburg with Jim. I knew that Widow Douglas would adopt me again, and try to civilize me. I'd been there before and I didn't want to go back. Maybe you've realized by now that I'm not the civilized type.

I'm not the type to stay in one place either.

A wind was picking up, and the raft began to pull from the shore. It wanted to get moving again, and so did I.

With a sad smile, I said goodbye to Tom and Jim, and then I set off in search of new adventures.

The Strange Case of
Dr. Jekyll and Mr. Hyde

Mr. Hyde roamed the streets in Victorian times, where life was respectable on the surface but dark and dangerous underneath. Robert Louis Stevenson, the author, may have been inspired by a man named William Brodie, who lived a century earlier: highly respected cabinet maker and master craftsman by day, but burglar by night...

Chapter 1

The story
of the door

It was a cold night in London. The full moon hung
low over the city's rickety rooftops, and wisps of
fog floated like ghosts through the squalid streets.
Two men strode side by side along a lamplit lane,
their footsteps echoing around the old walls. Their
names were Mr. Utterson and Mr. Enfield. They
walked together every Sunday, but they rarely spoke.

Until this night.

"You see that door?" Enfield said, prodding his
cane towards a dark doorway. "I know a strange
story about that door."

Utterson's bushy eyebrows rose in interest. "Go
on," he urged.

"It was a drizzly night last month," Enfield continued. "I was just leaving a tavern nearby, when a man came charging over the cobbles, so fast he ran straight into a little girl coming from the other direction. The poor child screamed, but the fellow simply trampled over her and kept running."

"Surely it was an accident?" Utterson said.

"Hardly," Enfield scoffed. "Utterson, the man laughed. I hear it in my head even now – a terrible, high-pitched cackle that sent a shiver down my spine."

"What did you do?" Utterson asked.

"Well, I set off after the man and tackled him. But when I saw his face, I wished I hadn't. His eyes were so dark they were almost black, and his mouth was twisted into a sinister sneer. I swear he looked like the Devil himself."

"Come now Enfield," Utterson laughed. "Surely you exaggerate?"

"I am not sure that I do, Utterson. The very sight of this man made my stomach turn. Still, I composed myself and dragged him back to the scene of his crime. The girl was crying, and her family yelled for the police."

"How did the fellow react to that?"

"The man's face broke into a vicious smile. He told them that he wished to avoid a scene, and offered the family a hundred pounds to remain silent about the incident."

"Did they accept?" Utterson asked.

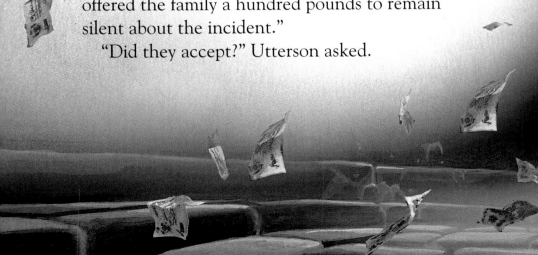

"They did. The sinister figure led us to this very house, where he produced the money and simply tossed it to the ground. Then he turned and slammed the door in our faces."

Enfield and Utterson continued strolling through the gaslight.

"I tell you Utterson," Enfield said, "never in my life have I met such a fiend. I am still haunted by the memory of his ghoulish face and brutal manner."

Utterson smiled at his friend's dramatic descriptions. "I shall be careful to avoid him," he replied. "Did he give you his name?"

"He did. His name was Edward Hyde."

Utterson's smile disappeared. "Hyde?" he said. "Are you quite sure?"

"Does the name mean something to you?"

"No," Utterson muttered, "that name means nothing to me."

But Utterson was lying. The name Edward Hyde haunted him too, but for a very different reason...

Chapter 2

The search for Mr. Hyde

That evening, Utterson sat in his house beside a crackling fire, gazing at a document in his hand. Utterson was a lawyer and the document he held was a will – the Last Will and Testament he had written for his close friend Dr. Henry Jekyll. Its final line had occupied his thoughts for months, but never more so than tonight...

In the event of my death or disappearance, all of my possessions are to pass into the hands of Mr. Edward Hyde.

Utterson had known Henry for most of his life, but had never heard the name Hyde before he read it in this will. And now here Hyde was again, in Enfield's terrible tale. What hold did such a fiend have over poor Henry?

"If anyone knows," Utterson thought, "it will be Lanyon."

An hour later, he arrived at the house of his friend, Hastie Lanyon, a red-faced doctor with slicked silver hair. They sipped wine and spoke happily of old times. He and Lanyon were university

friends, where they had both known Henry Jekyll.

"Did Henry ever mention a friend of his to you Lanyon?" Utterson asked. "He's a man named Edward Hyde."

"Hyde?" Lanyon said. "No, never heard of him. But I have not spoken to Henry for almost a year. We might both be doctors, but he began to speak such unscientific balderdash that I feared he had lost his mind. Now, let us talk of a happier subject..."

But all Utterson could think of was that sinister name in Henry Jekyll's will. "If he is Mr. Hyde," the lawyer decided, "then I shall be Mr. Seek."

From that night on, Utterson began to haunt the door that Enfield had shown him. Before work in the morning and after work at night, he hid in an alley and waited for a glimpse of the mysterious fiend.

At last, his patience was rewarded. Footsteps echoed along the foggy street. A hunched figure emerged from the gloom.

Utterson stepped out, blocking the man's path. "Mr. Hyde I think?" he said.

The man shrank back with a hissing intake of breath. His face remained hidden under the shadow of his crooked top hat.

"How do you know me?" he snapped.

"First," Utterson asked, "will you please let me see your face?"

Hyde hesitated, and then stepped closer to the street lamp. Utterson shivered when he saw the man in the light. It was hard to say what was wrong with him, just that there was something evil about his face. A line of spit hung from his mouth as he kept grinding his rotten teeth.

"Now," Hyde snarled. "Answer my question: how you know me?"

"Henry Jekyll gave me your address."

At this, Hyde broke into a savage laugh. He barged past Utterson, knocking the lawyer to the ground. The door slammed behind him as he disappeared into the house.

Utterson sat on the cobbles, trying to calm his hammering heart. Poor Henry, he thought. What can this devil have over him?

Chapter 3
Visiting Dr. Jekyll

Utterson barely slept that night. The leering face of Edward Hyde haunted his dreams. He saw those burning eyes and that cruel, sneering smile. The bedroom rang with the man's mocking laugh.

The following morning, he took a carriage to Henry Jekyll's house, a marble-stepped mansion with flowers hanging by the door. Inside, the doctor greeted Utterson with a friendly handshake and beaming smile.

As they ate breakfast together, Utterson studied his old friend. He was the same age as Utterson and Lanyon, but always seemed ten years younger. He certainly didn't look like a man stalked by a sinister enemy. But Utterson had to be sure...

"I want to talk about that will of yours," he announced over coffee.

Jekyll's smile vanished. "I asked you never to speak of it Utterson," he said.

"And I hoped not to," Utterson told him. "Except I have since heard more about this man Edward Hyde. Henry, what I heard was abominable."

"I am aware that you met him," Jekyll said, "and that he was uncivil to you."

"Uncivil? This man is a fiend Henry. And yet you have left him your entire fortune in your will. Tell me what hold he has over you."

Jekyll rose. The firelight cast his shadow long and monstrous across the wall.

"I cannot tell you," he said. "All I can say is that I fear there will soon come a time when I am no longer here. In that case, promise me you will give everything I own to Edward Hyde. Help me Utterson, if not as my lawyer, then as my friend."

How could Utterson refuse?

Picking up his hat and cane, he left the doctor alone. "I can't pretend I shall ever like Hyde," he said as he went. "But I promise."

Chapter 4
An inspector calls

Utterson agreed to let the issue of Hyde drop, but a few months later it thrust itself back into his life in a chilling manner.

It was a blustery Wednesday night when Utterson was woken by a knock on his front door. He lit a candle and carried the flickering light to the entrance. A police inspector stood outside with a grim look on his face.

"Mr. Utterson?" he asked. "I have a dark story to tell you."

Utterson lit a fire, as the inspector sat down and began his tale.

"It began across London," the inspector said, "as a maidservant looked out of her window before she slept. She saw an elderly gentleman who had lost his way in the night. The maid was about to offer directions, when another fellow came towards him, a man she describes as short and hunched."

A shiver ran down Utterson's spine. "Go on," he said.

"Well," the inspector continued, "all of a sudden this fellow broke into a rage. He struck the old man to the ground, and rained blows upon him with his cane. At the sight of such a terrible thing, the poor maid fainted."

"And the old man?"

"He is dead," the inspector said. "It is murder, Mr. Utterson."

The inspector reached into his coat pocket. He brought out the broken end of a walking cane. "Do you recognize this?" he asked.

Utterson did. It was a cane he had given to Henry Jekyll years ago. Inscribed on the handle was a message:

To Henry, from your friend Gabriel Utterson.

"So you see why I have come to you," the inspector said. "This was the murderer's stick. Who is this man 'Henry'?"

"It is Henry Jekyll."

"Then he is our killer."

"No," Utterson insisted, "Jekyll is a tall man. The maid described someone short. Inspector, I think I know the real name of the murderer. It is Edward Hyde, and I will gladly take you to his house."

The hunt was on.

The inspector marched behind Utterson as the

first glimmers of daylight lit the empty streets. Soon, they arrived in that dismal district, and at that decrepit door. Hyde's door.

The inspector pounded on it with his fist. "Edward Hyde!" he called. "I demand to speak to you."

No reply. The door creaked open on its rusty hinges. Utterson stepped back, happy to let the inspector lead the way inside.

It was morning outside, but the house was dark and dingy within. Drawers hung open and clothes lay strewn across the floor. Among them, Utterson spotted shirts and jackets belonging to Henry Jekyll.

"So... Hyde is a thief as well as a murderer," he whispered.

The inspector gestured for him to be quiet, as they crept deeper into the house. A fire crackled in the drawing room, but there was no one home.

"Looks like we have missed our man," Utterson observed.

The inspector picked something up from the floor. It was the other half of the broken walking stick. He raised the evidence triumphantly. "The murder weapon," he declared. "We have Mr. Hyde now."

Chapter 5

The incident of the letter

It was late afternoon by the time Utterson arrived at Henry Jekyll's house. The doctor's butler, Poole, greeted him with a worried frown.

"My master is in sir," he said, "but he is in very strange spirits."

Poole led Utterson to a laboratory at the back of the house. Light fell dimly through a crack in the curtains, illuminating a clutter of test tubes, strange potions in jars and powders corked in bottles.

Henry Jekyll was slumped in an armchair. His eyes were red and his skin had a feverish flush.

"Have you heard the news about your friend Hyde?" Utterson asked. "The police are searching for him across London."

Jekyll groaned in despair. "Utterson, I swear that I am done with Edward Hyde. Mark my words, that terrible man will never be heard from again. But there is one last thing..."

Jekyll held up a crumpled sheet of paper. The page trembled in his hand. "A messenger brought this letter today from Hyde," he said. "It says that he has run away and will never return. Do with it what you want, old friend."

"And what about your will, Henry? Should I remove Hyde's name from that document?"

Jekyll stared up at the dusky light leaking between the curtains. Utterson saw a look of desperate sadness in his friend's eyes.

"No," Jekyll said finally. "Leave the will as it is. Just in case..."

With that, the doctor sank into his chair, covering his face with his hands.

As he left the house, Utterson turned to the butler. "Poole?" he asked. "There was a letter delivered today. Did you see what the messenger looked like?"

Poole looked puzzled. "We have received no letters today sir," he said.

A dark thought entered Utterson's mind. He took Hyde's letter from his pocket and folded the bottom to conceal the sender's name. "Tell me Poole," he asked, "do you recognize this handwriting?"

Poole studied the page closely, and then nodded. "It looks different sir. But I would swear that this letter was written by Dr. Jekyll."

Utterson stumbled into the dusky streets, his mind reeling. Could it be possible? Could Henry Jekyll be covering for a murderer?

Chapter 6

The face at the window

Time ran on, and the hunt for Edward Hyde continued all over London. Thousands of pounds were offered in reward. But he had no family, and no photographs had ever been taken of him. Those who had seen his face found that they could not really describe him, other than to agree that he was a detestable-looking man.

As the weeks passed, Utterson thought less of Hyde, and more of Henry, who had become a new man. The doctor invited Utterson and Lanyon for dinner, and the three friends talked and laughed about old times. It was as if a dark cloud had lifted from over him.

Then, two months later, the cloud returned. It was a crisp January evening, and Utterson was on one of his walks through the city. He decided to pay Henry a visit.

But when he reached the doctor's house, Poole wouldn't let him in. "My master is confined to the house today," the butler said.

"Is he sick?" Utterson asked.

"Sir," Poole said, his face darkening, "I cannot say what is wrong with him."

Worried, Utterson marched around to the back of the house. He called to the laboratory window, "Henry! Are you unwell?"

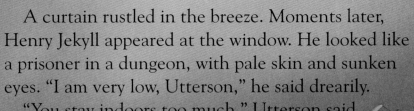

Dr. Jekyll and Mr. Hyde

A curtain rustled in the breeze. Moments later, Henry Jekyll appeared at the window. He looked like a prisoner in a dungeon, with pale skin and sunken eyes. "I am very low, Utterson," he said drearily.

"You stay indoors too much," Utterson said. "Get your hat and come for a walk."

Jekyll smiled sadly. "You are a good friend, Utterson," he said, "but I am afraid we can never meet again. From now on I intend to remain confined to my house."

"My dear chap, whatever for?"

"I have brought upon myself a punishment I cannot name. Ask Lanyon, he will tell you..."

Before Utterson could reply, Jekyll gave a terrific cry. He gritted his teeth and bent over, as if fighting some terrible pain. But the pain was too much.

The doctor collapsed back, clutching his stomach and crying out again.

Utterson heard a table crash over, and glass smash. Then, suddenly, the window slammed shut.

"Henry..." Utterson whispered. "What has become of you?"

He rushed to Lanyon's house. But there, too, he found his friend unwell.

Lanyon lay in bed, the blanket pulled up to his chin. Each time a door creaked or a window rattled in the wind, the doctor's eyes darted around the room. It seemed as if the man's nerves had been completely shattered.

"I have had a shock, Utterson," he said in a trembling voice, "from which I fear I shall never, ever recover."

"But Henry is ill too," Utterson said. "Have you seen him?"

A whimper escaped Lanyon's lips, and he sank deeper under his covers. "I wish to hear no more of Dr. Jekyll," he said, spitting the name like poison.

"But Lanyon," Utterson protested, "we three are old friends. I fear that Henry needs our help."

Lanyon gave a hollow laugh, which turned into a hacking cough. "Sit down Utterson," he said, "and I will tell you a story about our friend Henry Jekyll, and the help that I have *already* given him."

Utterson drew a chair closer as Hastie Lanyon began his tale...

Chapter 7
Dr. Lanyon's tale

"Four days ago," Lanyon told Utterson, "I was sitting alone at home when a messenger brought a letter. It was from Henry Jekyll."

Dear Hastie,

I beg you to help me. Upon receipt of this letter, proceed directly to the laboratory in my house. Remove the top drawer from the desk and carry it back to your home. At midnight, a man will come to collect it. Give it to him and ask no questions.

Please Lanyon, do as I ask! My life depends upon it.

Your friend, Henry.

"A strange request," Utterson said. "Did you carry it out?"

"How could I not?" Lanyon replied. "I took a carriage straight to Henry's house, where Poole let me into the laboratory. The room was in a terrible state, Utterson.

There were test tubes smashed across the floor, powders and potions spilled over desks, and notebooks scribbled with the results of failed experiments. More and more I feared that Henry Jekyll had lost his mind."

"But you found the drawer he mentioned in his letter?" Utterson asked.

"I did. It contained several jars of powder that looked like salt, but smelled unlike anything I have known. Just one sniff of the foul chemicals made me dizzy."

"Did you bring the drawer back here, as Henry asked?"

"I wish I had not Utterson. For what happened next has left me a broken man."

"Go on..."

"This was obviously a secret matter," Lanyon said, "so I sent my servants to bed and awaited the arrival of Henry's mysterious visitor. The chimes of midnight had barely struck when there came a fierce knock on my door. A dwarfish figure stood silhouetted in the porch light. He seemed agitated, unable to stand still.

'Have you got it?' the man snarled.

'Won't you come inside first?' I asked.

"The man shuffled into the light. Utterson, he was a repugnant figure. He kept grinding his teeth and muttering furiously to himself."

Utterson pulled his chair even closer to Lanyon's bed. "Grinding his teeth?" he repeated. "This man sounds like Edward Hyde."

"That was my fear too," replied Lanyon. "I wished then that I had not invited the ghastly individual into my house."

"What did he do next?" Utterson asked.

"He grew angry, Utterson.

'Where is it?' he growled. 'Where is the drawer? Tell me!'

'Compose yourself sir,' I told him. 'The drawer is over there.'

The man sprang at it with ferocious relish. A hideous grin spread across his face as he opened one of the jars of powder.

'Yes,' he said, hissing the word like a snake. 'Now, give me a glass of water,' he demanded."

"You gave it to him?" Utterson asked.

"I am not ashamed to say that I was scared, Utterson. I simply wanted the man gone. So I fetched him the water, and he poured the powder

into the glass. The mixture bubbled and frothed. Vile-smelling fumes swirled into the air. Another evil smile spread across the man's face.

'And now,' the man said, 'I suggest you leave.'

'Not a chance,' I told him, acting calmer than I felt. 'I have gone too far in this not to see the end.'

The man grew angry, but he couldn't wait... He
drank the revolting potion in one gulp. I have never
seen anything like it. His face twisted with pain.
His eyes rolled to the limits of their sockets. With
a blood-curdling scream, he collapsed to the floor,
where he lay curled up and moaning.

Finally he rose, careful to keep his back to me so
I couldn't see his face. He seemed taller somehow,
less agitated.

'Are you well?' I asked him.

Suddenly, he turned and barged past me for the door. But before he escaped into the night, I caught a glimpse of the man's face in the porch light. I... I..."

Lanyon scrunched his eyes shut and shuddered, haunted by the memory.

"What did you see?" Utterson asked.

"What I saw, Utterson, what I saw, was the face of Henry Jekyll!"

Chapter 8

The last night

Wind lashed at Utterson's face as he ran full pelt through the streets. Terrible thoughts raced through his mind. Could Lanyon's tale be true? Could Henry Jekyll and Edward Hyde really be the same person?

No! He refused to believe it. Surely Lanyon had lost his mind as well. But he had to find out. He reached Henry's house and hammered on the door.

Poole answered. A candle trembled in the butler's hand. His face was ghostly pale.

"Mr. Utterson," he gasped. "I am so glad you're here. I fear that my master has been murdered."

Tingling with fear, Utterson followed Poole into the house. He saw Jekyll's other servants cowering together by the fire. Something diabolical had indeed happened here. More than ever, Utterson was determined to get to the bottom of it.

Raising his shaky light, Poole led Utterson to Jekyll's laboratory. The door was locked, but Utterson heard someone moving inside.

"You saw Dr. Jekyll go into this room?" he asked the butler.

"As clear as day sir," Poole replied. "But soon after, I heard a piercing scream and the sound of smashing glass. Ever since, the door has been locked."

"Jekyll?" Utterson called, banging on the door. "I demand to see you."

"Go away," came the reply. "Please Utterson, just go away!"

Utterson felt a shiver of terror. That wasn't Jekyll's voice. It was Hyde.

"Stand back Poole," Utterson demanded.

"I'll smash my way in."

Poole stepped back as the lawyer launched forward, smashing the laboratory door with his shoulder – once... twice... three times.

With each thunderous blow, the men heard another desperate cry from inside.

"Please Utterson! Have mercy!"

The door crashed open and Utterson burst inside, his walking cane raised and ready to strike. But there was no need for the weapon.

Lying on the floor in a twisted heap, was the body of Edward Hyde. A bottle of red liquid rolled from the murderer's lifeless hand.

"Poison," Utterson said. "The fiend has taken his own life."

"Look sir," Poole said, examining a sheet of paper on the desk. "A note from Dr. Jekyll. It is addressed to you."

Utterson read the first line.

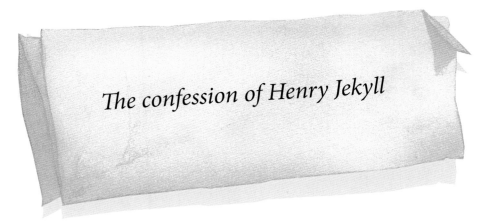

The confession of Henry Jekyll

Utterson stared at the corpse on the floor. Was Lanyon telling the truth? Could this man be his friend Henry too? The letter trembled in his hand as he began to read...

Chapter 9

The confession of Henry Jekyll

My dear Utterson,
    Now that my life reaches its end, the time has come to tell you everything about Henry Jekyll and Edward Hyde.

Of me you already know much. I strived to be a kind man and a good doctor. But more and more I grew troubled by the violence I witnessed in my work, the wounds from guns, knives, and bloody battles.

Dr. Jekyll and Mr. Hyde

I became convinced that all men were not truly one, but truly two – good and evil. I was determined to find a way to separate the two characters.

At night I experimented with chemicals, creating a potion that I hoped would rid man of his capacity for evil.

One night, I drank it.

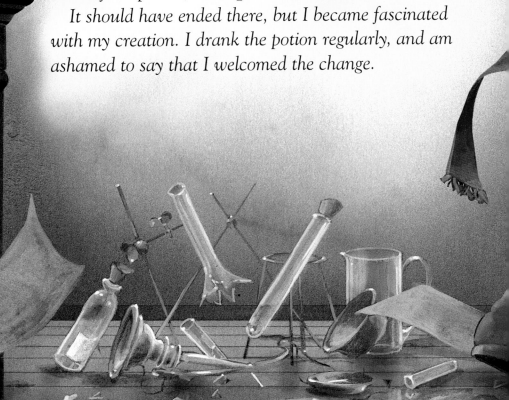

You have seen for yourself how the potion affected my body, Utterson, but you have not felt the indescribable pains. I felt a grinding in my bones, a sickness in my stomach. A terrible change came over me.

When I finally looked in a mirror, it wasn't Henry Jekyll that I saw, but a hideous, grinning stranger. This man told me his name was Edward Hyde.

I knew that Hyde was pure evil. So I quickly drank more of the potion, and again I became Henry Jekyll.

It should have ended there, but I became fascinated with my creation. I drank the potion regularly, and am ashamed to say that I welcomed the change.

Dr. Jekyll and Mr. Hyde

At night I stalked the streets as Edward Hyde. I felt alive, Utterson, I felt truly alive!

But gradually, Hyde began to take control of me. I began to change into him without even taking the potion. Fearing he would consume me completely, I had you write that will leaving everything I owned to Hyde. I even bought him his own house.

Hyde's evil grew worse and worse. He barged into men, cursed at women and trampled that young girl in the street. I knew I should put an end to him, but it was as if I was addicted to the dark side of his nature.

Then, one night, Hyde went too far – and murdered that poor man.

Suddenly all of London was hunting for Hyde. I began to take double and triple doses of the potion to stop myself from becoming him. I knew it might kill me, but I was desperate.

For three months, it succeeded. As you will remember Utterson, I became a new man. I was happy again. But it was not to last! One morning, as I walked in the park, I was wracked by the pains of the change. A moment later, I was Hyde again.

Dr. Jekyll and Mr. Hyde

Hyde knew that he would be hanged if he was caught. So he turned to Lanyon to help secure the powder from my house. I am sure the doctor has told you what happened next, and that has led you now to my house.

But it is too late to save me. I have run out of the powder that stops me from becoming Edward Hyde. Soon Hyde will take control of me forever. But before that can happen, I am resolved to take my own life with poison.

I have created a monster, and now I must slay it. Yes, I feel him stirring inside me now...

Goodbye then Utterson. You were a true friend. Henry Jekyll

"Sir?" Poole said.

Utterson flinched, crumpling the letter in his hands. He had been so lost in Jekyll's confession that he'd forgotten where he was.

He turned, gazing at the monster, Edward Hyde, lying dead on the floor.

This letter Utterson held would destroy Henry's reputation. He would be remembered as a monster. What had he once said?

"Help me Utterson, if not as my lawyer, then as my friend."

Utterson stepped to the fire and tossed Henry's confession onto the flames. Sparks crackled up the chimney, as shadows danced and darted around the laboratory walls.

"What about Dr. Jekyll sir?" Poole said.

"Henry Jekyll is gone, Poole," Utterson said. "He will never be seen again."

Then the lawyer turned and walked out into the night.

Kidnapped

In the middle of the 18th century, Scotland was fiercely divided. The clans (tribes) of the Highlands, in the north, were mainly Catholic, and hated the Protestant King, George II. In the south, most 'Lowlanders' supported the King. This is the story of a Lowlander, a Highlander and their incredible adventure.

Chapter 1
The House of Shaws

There is no finer sight than a Scottish valley on a clear summer morning. Blackbirds swoop through the dawn mist, and the sun lights up the heather as if the ground were sprinkled with a thousand diamonds.

But I was in mixed spirits that morning, as I walked from Edinburgh to the district of Cramond. My father had died just three weeks earlier. He left me a sealed letter, with an instruction on the front:

To be delivered to Ebenezer Balfour,
of the House of Shaws, by my son
David Balfour.

Kidnapped

David Balfour – that's me. And Ebenezer is my uncle. I'd never met him, but had heard that he was a rich lord. I hoped he might give me a new start in life. I dreamed of being a gentleman, with a title after my name.

But, when I reached my uncle's house later that day, my heart sank. It was a miserable building. All of the windows were broken, and crows perched like gargoyles on their crumbling ledges. Was this the place on which I had pinned my hopes?

I continued, determined to deliver my father's letter. No lights flickered inside, but a thin wisp of smoke rose from the crooked chimney.

I knocked on the door. At first, there was no reply. Then, to my horror, a gun poked through one of the windows – aimed at me!

A man's face appeared in the window – round and wrinkled, like a walnut. "Who are you?" he said, in a shrill voice.

"My name is David Balfour," I replied, hoping I sounded braver than I felt. "I have a letter for you from my father."

I noticed the gun shake in the man's grip.

"I'll...I'll let you in," he said. "Wait there."

The door creaked open on rusty hinges. A chill ran down my back when I saw the man properly. He looked like a ghost in rags – with pale skin, sunken eyes, and a long shirt that was tattered and filthy. I knew that this must be my uncle, because there were clearly no servants, nor anyone else, in his decrepit house.

"Come inside," he grunted.

He led me down a gloomy corridor and into a bare kitchen. A fire crackled in the hearth, but the room was icily cold. He offered me a bowl of porridge, which I ate hungrily.

"So, you've come after my money have you?" he croaked.

I rose from the table, angry at his accusation. "I am no beggar, sir! My father is dead, and I came with his letter."

As I spoke, I thought I saw my uncle smile. Was he pleased that his brother had died?

Suddenly, he snatched the letter from my hand. He read it quickly, then tossed it into the fire.

"Don't get upset, Davie," he said. "That letter asked me to look after you, and I shall. But first, you must sleep."

He showed me to a room that was even colder
than the kitchen. The walls glistened with damp,
and cockroaches scurried around the floor. But
before I could protest, he slammed the door and
locked me in.

"Good night, nephew!" he yelled.

I was too tired to complain. I pulled my coat
around me and curled up on the bed.

Chapter 2
Tricked!

I lay awake for most of the night, shivering from the cold and listening to the hollow moan of the wind over the hills.

Next morning, when I heard the door being unlocked, I was ready to shout at my uncle. But he gripped my arm with a wrinkly hand.

"I am sorry for last night, Davie," he said. "I mean to help you. You are family, after all."

Again, I saw a cunning smile flash across his face. I did not trust him at all.

Breakfast was another bowl of porridge. I was still too angry to speak to Ebenezer. Instead, I took a book from a shelf, and flicked through it as I ate. I was surprised to see an inscription at the front, written in my father's hand.

To my brother Ebenezer,
on his fifth birthday.

This confused me. I thought my father was Ebenezer's younger brother – how could he have written that well when he was so young?

Unless... Was my father older than Ebenezer? If so, then he should have inherited this estate. And that would mean that this house, and my uncle's money, belonged to me.

Ebenezer saw my frown as I read the inscription. "Give me that!" he shrieked. He sprang from his chair and snatched the book from my hands. Then he threw that into the fire as well.

"You don't trust me, Davie."

"I certainly do not," I replied, stiffly. "Are you even the true lord of this estate?"

My uncle winced. Had I offended him, or scared him with the truth?

"What nonsense!" he said. "You must come with me to Queensferry. We can visit my lawyer, Mr. Rankeillor. He knew your father, and will put your mind at rest."

"Very well," I declared. "Lead the way."

It was a long walk to
Queensferry, into a chilly wind.
I thought we were going to visit
the lawyer, but instead my uncle
led me to the town's docks. The
seafront bustled with activity, as
sailors prepared a ship for sea.

We stopped outside
a dingy tavern on the
edge of the wharf.

The Covenant

"I just have to take care of some business with the ship's captain," Ebenezer explained.

Inside, I watched my uncle meet with the captain – a big man with a brutal face, and tattoos on his arms. I wondered what sort of business Ebenezer could have with a man like that...

As I stood at the bar, the landlord eyed me suspiciously. "Did you come here with Ebenezer?" he said.

I told him that I did.

"Your face reminds me of his brother, Alexander," he replied.

He meant my father. "Did you know him?" I asked.

"Oh yes. Alexander was as good as Ebenezer is wicked. I heard that Ebenezer cheated him of his inheritance."

My suspicions were confirmed! And that meant the House of Shaws belonged to me. More than ever, I wanted to speak with this lawyer, Mr. Rankeillor. I set off from the tavern to find him.

As I marched along the dock, a voice called out. "Mr. Balfour!"

The captain strode from the inn. His face was red

and flustered. "Do you have a moment to talk?" he asked. He leaned closer, and I smelled the beer on his breath. "It's about your uncle. I think he means you harm."

"What harm?" I asked.

"I will tell you in private, on my ship."

He led me on board, as his crew loaded the last crates for their voyage. The ship swayed and the tall masts creaked and groaned.

"Now," I asked, "what harm does my uncle wish upon me?"

"This!" cried the captain.

Before I could react, he swung a plank at my head. I felt a sharp blow, like a thunderbolt, and collapsed to the deck. My head swirled. My vision swam. Through blurry eyes, I saw the sailors cast off the ship's ropes. We were going to sea!

Just as I began to pass out, I saw my uncle watching from the dock. A cruel smile spread across his wrinkled face.

"No," I gasped. "No..."

And then I saw nothing.

Chapter 3

The outlaw Alan Breck

For three days, I drifted in and out of consciousness, locked in the belly of the ship. I overheard the crew on the deck, and learned that we were headed for America, where I would be sold as a slave.

There was nothing I could do – I was too weak to fight the crew alone. Instead, I curled up on the floor, sobbing pathetically. I should have been the lord of an estate, but now I faced a life of misery.

Kidnapped

Once I had recovered, I was forced to work in the roundhouse – the cabin where the sailors ate. All day, I served the captain and his crew meals and poured them drinks.

At night, I was kept awake by the violent sway of the ship on the waves. By the fifth day of my capture, the waves had grown even higher. I heard the crew shout and curse, as they struggled against a storm.

Kidnapped

As I served the captain a drink, I sneaked a look at his sea chart. I was stunned to see how far the wind had forced us back – we were now only five miles from the coast of the Scottish Highlands.

Right at that moment, a mighty crash shook the wooden walls.

"We've hit a boat!" one of the crew yelled.

I rushed to the window, and was horrified to see a small dinghy sinking in the waves. There was no sign of its crew, except one man, who clung bravely to the front of our ship.

"Bring him aboard!" the captain ordered.

The man was rescued and brought into the roundhouse.

He was a striking figure, with broad shoulders and wide, twinkling eyes. He wore a flamboyant feathered hat and a plush velvet coat that was decorated with silver buttons. The buttons clinked against a sword at his side.

The clothes looked French, but the man was Scottish. I guessed that he was a rebel – one of the Highlanders who fought against the British king and his army in Scotland.

"My apologies for your boat," the captain said, although he didn't sound sorry at all.

"Save them for its crew," the man replied, "who are at the bottom of the sea. In return, you can land me on the shore."

I saw the captain glance greedily at a purse in the man's pocket. I knew then that he planned to trick this man, just as he had tricked me.

"I'll talk to my crew," said the captain.

As soon as we were alone, I poured the man a drink. I leaned close, lowering my voice to a whisper. "They're going to kill you," I said.

The man sipped the drink coolly. "I suspected as much," he said. "And will you stand with me?"

At last, here was my opportunity to escape. Highland rebels were famous for their courage. Perhaps, with this man's help, I actually stood a chance against the crew.

"I will," I said firmly.

The man grinned, and clapped me on the back. "Then I had better know your name."

"It is David Balfour, the true lord of the estate of Shaws."

I thought my title would impress him, but his grin grew wider.

"Well, David of the Shaws, my name is Alan Breck. But I'm afraid I don't have an estate to boast about."

I was embarrassed by his joke, but there was no time to worry about that now.

Alan Breck drew his sword. "How many sailors are there?" he asked.

"Fifteen," I told him. "They have swords, but

look... We have all the guns."

Alan's eyes lit up as I showed him the chest where the crew stored their firearms.

"Ha!" he said. "Maybe we will survive the night after all."

He handed me a pistol, but my hand trembled with fear, and I could barely hold the weapon.

Just then I heard the thump of feet on the deck, as the captain and his crew charged at the roundhouse.

"Be brave, David of the Shaws," cried Alan. "Here they come!"

Chapter 4
Shipwreck

There was a mighty roar, and the first sailor burst through the door. I had never experienced a battle before and I am ashamed to say that the man's savage cry made me freeze with fear.

But Alan didn't hesitate. He launched forward, whirling his sword. The steel blade glinted in the lamplight as he sunk the weapon deep into the man's chest.

More of the crew stormed inside, and I knew I had to act. I gathered my courage, gripped my pistol and fired.

BOOM!

Blood sprayed everywhere and one of the sailors staggered back, clutching his arm.

Alan charged again, striking out with his sword. There was a clash of steel and cries from the crew.

Kidnapped

Quickly, I reloaded the gun. My next shot hit the wall, but it was enough to scare the attackers away. They turned and fled, dragging their dead crewmate with them.

My ears still rang from the gunshots. The weapon slipped from my hand and clattered to the floor. I couldn't stop shaking.

Alan, though, looked delighted. He threw his arms around me in a tight hug. "You stood beside me in battle, Davie," he said. "I will never forget that. But it's not over yet. They'll soon be back."

I pulled on my coat, and we sat against the wall, waiting for the next attack. Alan spoke proudly about his life. He told me that he was from a clan named the Stewarts, who fought against King George and his army.

I felt embarrassed. I was from the Lowlands of Scotland, where most people supported the King.

Alan's face grew dark. "I tell you Davie," he said. "I curse any Highland clan that helps the King. But the person I hate the most is the Red Fox – a Highlander who works for the King's army. He plans to force every Stewart from their home and steal their land. You would know the Red Fox if you saw him, Davie, for he has long, flame-red hair."

He gripped the handle of his sword. "If I had the chance, I would murder that scoundrel right now."

The force in Alan's words startled me. He must have noticed, for his hand rose and gripped my shoulder reassuringly.

"The Stewarts are loyal to each other, Davie," he said. "And now that we have fought together, they'll be loyal to you, too."

With his sword, he cut one of the buttons from his coat. He placed it in my hand, and I saw that it was decorated with an intricate, swirling pattern.

"Wherever you go in the Scottish Highlands," he told me, "show that button, and my friends will help you."

Again, I felt my face redden with shame. I had hoped that a title after my name would make people respect me. All Alan needed to earn respect was a button.

I was about to thank him when the captain burst back into the roundhouse. His face had turned white with fear.

"The ship is in grave danger," he cried. "We need your help to control the sails or we will be wrecked on the rocks."

Alan and I rushed outside, just as a huge wave washed over the deck. The fierce wind was already tearing the sails to shreds, and the ship lurched violently on the water.

In the moonlight, I saw that we were close to the coast. But, all around us, jagged rocks rose from the water, like the fangs of a giant sea monster.

"Hold on for your life, Davie!" Alan cried.

The ship slammed against the rocks. Wood shattered. Waves crashed. And we were all flung into the sea.

Kidnapped

The dark water swallowed me, and then spat me back up. In a flash of lightning, I saw sailors drowning, and the wreck of the ship smashing against the rocks.

"Alan!" I screamed. But my cry was lost to a roar of thunder.

I grasped a plank, and clung on for my life. Then I kicked my legs as hard as I could until I felt sand under my feet. Shaking from cold and fear, I crawled onto the beach and collapsed...

Chapter 5
The Red Fox

Whmen I woke, the storm had passed and
sunlight dazzled my eyes. Wreckage from the
ship was strewn across the beach, but I could see no
other survivors.

My lips were parched and hunger gnawed at my
belly. I felt so miserable and alone. But, far inland,
a trail of smoke rose into the sky. Was it coming from
a house?

Kidnapped

As I staggered closer, I saw that it was more like a hut, in the middle of a wide, empty moor. A toothless old man sat outside, puffing on a pipe.

"Help!" I groaned. "My ship has been wrecked. Have you seen any other survivors?"

He plucked the pipe from his mouth, and blew a cloud of smoke. "Perhaps," he said.

I understood his reply. Alan Breck was a wanted outlaw. If this man was his friend, he would be wary of telling people that he'd seen him here.

I remembered Alan's button and fished it out from my pocket.

The moment he saw it, the old man grinned. "The boy with the silver button!" he said.

"Where is Alan?" I asked eagerly.

"He has gone into the Highlands to hide. He told me that you might pass. Come inside and eat!"

I must have thanked that man a hundred times, as he stoked the fire to get me warm, and gave me hot porridge.

As I ate, I stared into the fire, and thought of my evil uncle. I was determined to get revenge against him, and claim my rightful inheritance. To do so, I would have to find the lawyer, Mr. Rankeillor, and hope that he believed my story. He lived in Queensferry, and that was a long walk from here, across wild Highland countryside. I wasn't sure that I was tough enough for that sort of journey, but I had to try.

Kidnapped

The next day, I set off. Wrapped in a blanket, I tramped across fields of heather, and vast, desolate moors. The sky darkened and freezing rain soaked my clothes. When the sun came out, biting flies swarmed around my face.

The walk was even harder than I had feared. But, wherever I showed Alan's button, I was greeted with warmth. His friends gave me food, drink and beds by crackling fires.

As my journey went on, I began to feel more and more ashamed. I had always believed that Highlanders were wild people, who needed to be tamed. But, so far, I had only met kindness.

Kidnapped

One morning, I came to some woods at the bottom of a craggy hill. A line of English soldiers marched along the path, brass buttons gleaming on their coats. They were led by a burly man, whose face was as red as his long, shaggy hair.

I realized with a shudder that this was the man that Alan had told me about – the Red Fox. The Red Fox and the soldiers were hunting for people who opposed King George, to throw them from their homes.

I stepped aside, hoping they would march past. But the Red Fox ordered the soldiers to stop. Then he stepped up to me, and jabbed me in the chest.

"You!" he said, with a sneer. "Are you loyal to the King, or to the rebels?"

I didn't know what to say. I was proud to be a friend of the rebel Alan Breck, but if I said so now, I would be arrested. Before I could answer...

BOOM!

A gunshot rang out from the woods. The Red Fox staggered back and collapsed.

"He's been murdered!" cried a soldier.

A dark figure raced away between the trees. It was the killer! Several soldiers set off after him, but the others turned and aimed their rifles at me.

"This man must be the killer's accomplice," one of them said.

Another soldier tried to grab me, but I dodged his grasp. I wanted to tell them I was innocent, but knew they wouldn't listen.

Instead, I fled between the trees. Bullets whizzed past my head, missing me by inches. Suddenly, it seemed as if there were soldiers everywhere. I was breathless with fear, barely able to think.

A hand grasped my arm. I cried out and turned to fight, and couldn't believe who I saw – Alan!

Kidnapped

He pulled me behind a rock, just as several
soldiers charged past, running deeper into the
woods. Then Alan burst from our hiding place and
raced up the hill. "Come on, Davie," he called.

I ran after him, scrambling over rocks. We stopped at the top of the hill and lay down to catch our breath. Now that we were safe, my fear turned into anger. "Did you murder the Red Fox?" I demanded.

"It wasn't me," Alan said. "I came back to find you, Davie. I hated the Red Fox, but killing him would only bring more trouble upon my clan."

I could see in his eyes that he was telling the truth. "Then who did kill him?"

"I didn't see," Alan replied.

I knew that he was lying to protect the killer. Although I didn't approve, I respected his loyalty to his fellow outlaws.

"You are an outlaw too now, Davie," Alan told me. "Luckily the soldiers do not know your name. We must go south, to your part of Scotland, so you can reclaim your estate. Then you can help me find a ship to take me to France."

He gripped my arm firmly. "It won't be easy," he warned. "The English soldiers will hunt us like wild animals. Are you ready?"

I breathed in deeply, gathering what little courage I had left. "I am," I said.

Chapter 6
On the run

We hid during the day, in case the army spotted us. Then we moved at night, side-by-side through the misty moonlight. Sometimes we ran, sometimes we walked – up rocky hills, across fierce rivers, and along valleys strewn with granite boulders. Around us, wild mountains rose into the starry sky.

Kidnapped

We slept for one day in a cave at the base of a mountain. For another day, we hid at the top of a hill and watched soldiers in the valley below. They were searching for us.

The next night, we climbed one mountain after another, struggling against bitter winds. I felt dizzy with tiredness, but I kept going, determined not to let Alan down.

By sunrise, we reached a vast moor – a sea of purple heather. It was too light to keep going, but there was nowhere to hide.

"This is a dangerous place to stop," Alan muttered. "You sleep first, Davie. I will keep watch."

I slept for three hours, curled up like a baby in the prickly heather. Alan woke me around noon, when the sun was directly overhead.

"Now you keep watch," he whispered.

He lay back and, seconds later, he was snoring.

I sat beside him and tried to stay awake. But my eyes felt so heavy. The soft drone of the bees lulled me into a slumber... and I closed my eyes.

I jolted awake, and almost cried out in anger. I had broken Alan's trust and fallen asleep. And then I saw the soldiers!

A dozen men on horseback rode slowly in our direction, spread out across the moor.

I woke Alan, and felt so ashamed. He knew I had fallen asleep, but he didn't mention it.

"Over there," he said, spotting a forest on the
other side of the moor. "If we can reach those trees,
we might be safe."

But, to do so, we would have to pass right in front
of the soldiers...

Kidnapped

We didn't dare stand up. Instead, we slid on our stomachs like snakes. Jagged stones cut our bellies, and the spiky heather scratched our faces.

We got closer to the woods, but the soldiers got closer to us, too.

Now one of them was only twenty yards away...

Now he was ten yards from us...

My heart pounded so hard I was sure it would give us away. But the horse kept riding – the soldier didn't see us.

"Now!" Alan whispered.

We rose and sprinted into the woods. We ran and ran, stumbling like old men. We didn't stop until the sun disappeared from the sky and darkness settled again over the Highlands.

Finally, we flopped into the long grass.

"We're safe now," Alan wheezed.

I lay beside him, my legs aching with exhaustion. We were still alive, but only just. And I feared there were more dangers ahead.

Chapter 7
Back home

We rested for a day, to recover our strength. Then we hiked again through the night. The weather grew even colder, but I felt stronger with each step. We had left the Highlands and entered the Scottish Lowlands. I was close to home.

"We're not safe yet, Davie," Alan warned. "We need to find the lawyer, Mr. Rankeillor, and hope that he believes your story."

By morning, we had reached Queensferry. We rested on the roadside, watching smoke rise in lazy lines from the chimneys of the stone houses.

We were both wanted outlaws and risked being caught if we entered a town. But I still felt ashamed for letting Alan down before, and knew this was my chance to make it up to him.

"I'll go," I said. "You stay here, where it's safe."

Kidnapped

Alan knew not to argue. He grasped my shoulder and smiled warmly. "I love you like a brother, Davie. Good luck!"

Kidnapped

My heart thumped as I entered Queensferry. It was an elegant market town, so I stood out in my dirty clothes. But, finally, I found the house I was looking for.

I knocked on the door, and was greeted by a man in a powdered wig and spectacles.

It was Mr. Rankeillor. "Can I help?" he asked.

At first, I was too scared to speak. If I told this lawyer my story, he might have me arrested. But I remembered Alan's courage in the Highlands, and stood up straight.

"My name is David Balfour," I declared. "I am the true lord of the House of Shaws."

The lawyer's eyes widened. "You had better come in," he said.

He led me into a dusty room, with books on shelves around the walls. "Now, tell me your story," he said, as he sat behind a desk.

So, I told him everything that had happened – the shipwreck, the murder of the Red Fox, my journey through the Highlands, and how my uncle Ebenezer had cheated me of my inheritance.

After I had finished, Mr. Rankeillor sat in silence for a minute or two, with his eyes closed. It felt like an eternity...

Then he sprang from his seat, and smiled. "You have been on an epic journey, David," he said. "Why, you've trekked across half of Scotland!"

"You... You believe me?" I asked, fearing this was a trick.

"Of course I do! I know your uncle and I have no doubt that he is capable of such wickedness. I used to work for Ebenezer, until I discovered what a scoundrel he was."

I was so relieved to hear this that I had to sit down. "So what should I do?"

Mr. Rankeillor thought about it for a moment, and then his grin grew wider.

"You must plan a trick of your own on Ebenezer.

You need to make him admit his crime. But, for that, you will need help from someone very daring..."

Now I smiled too, for the first time in weeks. "I know just the person," I said.

Chapter 8
Revenge

Later that night, Alan Breck strolled casually to the front door of my uncle's crumbling mansion, and banged on the door.

Close by, I hid with Mr. Rankeillor in some bushes. Alan glanced over at us and gave a firm wink. I couldn't help grinning in reply – our plan was underway.

The door creaked open. I felt a flush of anger when I saw Uncle Ebenezer again, pointing his gun at Alan. But Mr. Rankeillor gripped my arm, urging me to stay hidden. We had to let Alan talk...

"Who are you?" my uncle demanded.

Alan smiled calmly. "I have come about David," he said.

Ebenezer's gun trembled, and his eyes twitched.

"D...David?" he stuttered.

"I am from the Isle of Mull," Alan said, repeating the story we had created. "There was a shipwreck there, and a survivor washed up on the beach. My clan have locked him in our castle's dungeon, and I am here to demand a ransom for his release."

Alan sounded so convincing that I almost believed his story myself.

"Keep him in your castle," Ebenezer said, with a cruel grin.

"We can't do that," Alan replied. "If you won't pay, then we will have to kill him. Is that really what you want?"

The smile spread wider across my uncle's face, and I knew he was thinking of saying yes. But he shook his head. "How much would I have to pay you to keep him locked up?" he asked.

"Well now..." Alan said. "How much did you pay for David to be kidnapped? That is what you did, isn't it?"

Ebenezer shrugged. "I did, and I'm not sorry either. I gave the captain twenty pounds. Is that enough for you?"

As soon as my uncle said this, Mr. Rankeillor leaped from our hiding place. "That is quite enough for me, Mr. Balfour!" he shouted.

Now I stepped into the moonlight too. "Good evening," I said.

Ebenezer's face turned as pale as the moon.

Kidnapped

My uncle knew he'd been tricked into confessing his crime. He stood in the doorway, like a man turned to stone.

We led him into the kitchen and seated him at
the table.

Mr. Rankeillor had prepared a document that
gave the house, and all of Ebenezer's money, to
me. My uncle knew that he had to sign it, or else
he would face prison. Once he had, we took him
upstairs and locked him in his bedroom.

Alan and Mr. Rankeillor poured drinks and we

celebrated our victory. I decided to let Ebenezer stay
here, although now I was the lord of this house. But
I didn't really care about having a title any more.
I knew, from my time with Alan, that it was a man's
actions that proved his worth.

Kidnapped

The next day, I walked with Alan to Edinburgh. My adventure was over, but he still had a long journey ahead. I gave him some money to pay for his voyage to France, and prayed that he would make it there safely.

We walked slowly, and in silence. As the sun set, we stopped on top of a hill and looked out across Edinburgh and the sea.

Alan took my hand. "Goodbye," he said, "David of the Shaws."

I cleared my throat, hoping Alan didn't hear the emotion in my voice. "Goodbye, Alan," I replied.

Kidnapped

As I watched him walk away, I thought of all the adventures we had been through together. I would miss my friend, the outlaw Alan Breck.

I felt so sad right then that I wanted to cry. But I knew Alan wouldn't approve. I was a man now, and I had to act like one. So I stood up straight, fastened my coat, and set off back to my new home.

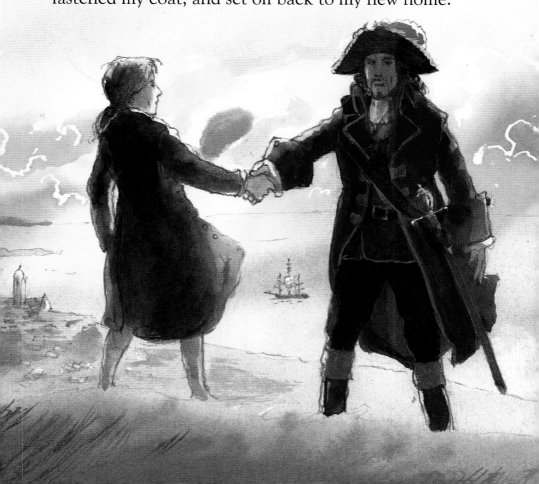

King Solomon's Mines

The author of this adventure – Henry Rider Haggard – spent many years working for the Lieutenant Governor of Natal in what is now South Africa. His experience of Britain's conflict with the Zulus and the First Boer War inspired several adventure stories such as this one.

Chapter 1

Lost in Africa

The most extraordinary adventure of my life began aboard a steamship sailing from Cape Town to Durban.

I had experienced many dangers during my time in Africa. But, as I strolled around the deck on that cool January night, little could have prepared me for the nerve-shattering perils that lay ahead.

"Excuse me, sir," came a booming voice from behind me. I turned to see a great bear of a man, broad-chested, with flowing golden hair and a fullsome beard. "But are you by any chance Mr. Allan Quatermain?" he asked.

"I am," I replied, cautiously.

The fellow seemed relieved. "My name is Sir Henry Curtis," he declared with a smile. "And this is my friend, Captain John Good." He gestured to a shorter, stout man beside him, who wore a monocle in his right eye that sparkled in the twilight.

"When I discovered you were on board, I had to speak with you," said Sir Henry. "If you would be kind enough to dine with us this evening, I will explain everything."

Over dinner, Sir Henry told me that he had come all the way from England in search of his brother.

"Three years ago, my brother and I argued, Mr. Quatermain. I needn't trouble you with the details, save that it ended with George setting off to southern Africa to make his fortune."

"Sir Henry has neither seen nor heard from him since," added Captain Good.

"I'm determined to bring my brother home and make amends," said Sir Henry.

"You have quite a reputation in this part of the world, Mr. Quatermain," said Good. "Our inquiries have led us to believe that you may have met Sir Henry's brother."

"Two years ago, when you were trading in the Transvaal?" prompted Sir Henry, eagerly.

I cast my mind back. "It's some time ago, gentlemen. Even so, I don't recall ever meeting a George Curtis..."

"We believe he was calling himself Neville at the time," interjected Good.

Something about this name struck a chord. "Yes, there was a fellow," I recalled. "He camped nearby for two weeks or so."

Sir Henry could hardly contain his excitement. "And what became of him, Mr. Quatermain? Did he tell you where he was headed?"

"Oh yes, gentlemen," I replied solemnly. The memory was only too clear now. "He was searching for King Solomon's Mines."

Chapter 2

The legend of the mines

"I first heard the legend of King Solomon's Mines about thirty years ago, from an old elephant hunter," I explained. "They are said to date back over two thousand years, and lie somewhere north of the Suliman Mountains."

"What was mined there?" asked Good.

"Diamonds, Captain," I replied. "More diamonds than any man has seen before or since – so the legend says."

"You don't believe it, then?" said Sir Henry.

"I might not have done, were it not for an incident some twenty years ago. I was out at Sitanda's Kraal, just north of where the Lukanga River meets the Kalukawe. One day, a Portuguese chap named Silvestre staggered into my camp. He'd come from the desert and was nothing but skin and bone."

Sir Henry looked aghast. "What had happened to the poor devil?" he asked.

"He'd tried to cross the desert and ran out of water," I replied, shuddering at the memory of that wretched figure. "But before he died, he handed me a map."

I took a sheet of paper from my pocket-book. "This is my translation of the original."

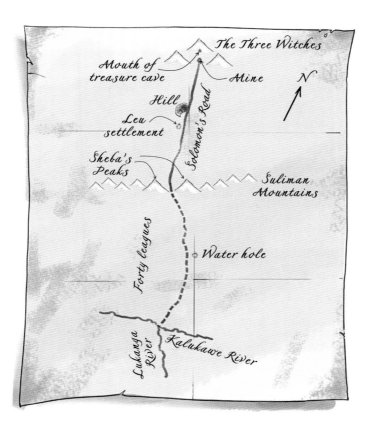

"Silvestre said the map was made by one of his ancestors," I went on. "This relative had made it to the mines, but died on the return journey, empty handed save for the map."

"So Sir Henry's brother was on the same mission as these Silvestres," sighed Good.

"It needn't mean that George has met with a similar fate," said Sir Henry.

"Before your brother set off, I gave his servant a note with the directions mentioned on the map," I explained. "That may have given him a chance."

Sir Henry shot Good a determined look. "Then we must go after George," he declared, "to King Solomon's Mines."

Good frowned. "We'll need a guide."

Sir Henry fixed me with a steely gaze. "Mr. Quatermain," he said, "will you join us?"

Chapter 3
The desert of danger

So it was, that, five months later, our party arrived at Sitanda's Kraal. It had been a thousand mile journey from Durban, the last three hundred on foot, due to deadly tsetse flies that had killed off our oxen.

On the way, I managed to teach Sir Henry and Captain Good some Zulu, and they had both become fairly proficient.

We had been joined on our mission by two servants I'd hired at Durban – a tough little bushman I knew named Ventvögel, and Umbopa, a tall, handsome-looking Zulu, a stranger to me, who'd offered his services out of the blue.

After a brief rest, we left Sitanda's Kraal and began our trek across the desert.

We decided to travel by night and rest by day, so as to reduce exposure to the scorching desert sun. The first daylight stop passed well enough, though I was glad of the large gourds of water we carried with us. We spent the time sleeping beneath the shade of a massive boulder, and by late afternoon we set off again.

By dawn the next day, we were ready to drop, but no sizeable shade presented itself.

Then Good had the notion of digging a pit and burying ourselves inside. It seemed worth a try, but even with sprigs cut from nearby karoo bushes to cover us, we could only withstand the discomfort for a few hours.

Slowly we trudged on and on, until we had covered some forty-five miles.

"Only another fifteen miles and we should reach the water hole on Silvestre's map," I gasped, my lips as parched as dry leaves.

But it seemed that luck was not on our side. At the spot where the water hole should have been, there was nothing but a massive sand hill. We slumped down despondently in the shade it offered, and sipped down our last few pathetic drops of liquid from the gourds.

As we slipped into unconsciousness, Umbopa spoke what we all feared. "If we can't find water, we shall all be dead before the moon rises tomorrow."

Chapter 4
Tragedy on the mountain

We slept as best we could, before waking with our torturous thirsts still raging. It was then that Ventvögel became agitated, pointing at a row of animal tracks in the sand.

"Springboks don't go far from water," he said, excitedly sniffing the air. "I can smell it, Mr. Quatermain. I can smell it!"

I couldn't see how. "There's not a drop of water in sight," I argued.

Sir Henry stroked his long beard thoughtfully. "Perhaps it's on *top* of the hill, Quatermain?" he suggested, looking upwards.

The idea hardly seemed credible, but we were too desperate to discount it. We scrambled up the sandy side of the mound until we reached the summit.

There, sure enough, was a small pool of water. How it came to be there I will never know, but thank heaven for it. We joyously drank, bathed and filled our water gourds. Then, as night fell, we set off once more, our spirits restored.

Ahead of us, we could make out the two enormous, snow-capped mountains that were Sheba's Peaks. Forty-eight hours later, we found ourselves on their lower slopes.

It soon became clear that these mighty peaks must once have been volcanoes. The ground beneath our feet was hardened lava now, which made the ascent a painful one.

As we got higher up, the air became cooler and

cooler. At first, this came as a relief after the baking heat of the desert. But as we began to encounter patches of snow, we realized that we had merely exchanged one danger for another.

Within a couple of days, the temperature had dropped to something like ten or fifteen degrees below zero. By now, our rations of dried meat were gone, and it seemed as though we had escaped death by thirst only to die of hunger.

As dusk approached one night, Umbopa grabbed Good's arm and pointed to what appeared to be a hole in the snow. "A cave!" he cried.

We piled into the tiny cavern and huddled together for warmth. We sat for hour after hour

through that bitter night, the frost eating into our miserable, starved carcasses.

Ventvögel's back was pressed against mine and, as the night wore on, it seemed to get colder and colder, till at last it was like ice.

The next morning, as the sun's rays reached the mouth of the cave, they illuminated a terrible sight. There sat the poor fellow, totally immobile, frozen to death.

Our spirits were laid low after this tragic loss. But we had no choice but to leave our loyal friend to his eternal vigil, and set off once again on our mission.

We hadn't gone more than half a mile when, some five hundred yards beneath us, at the end of a long slope of snow, we saw a patch of green grass, through which a stream was running. By the stream stood a group of antelopes, basking in the morning sun. A short while later, we were enjoying our first fresh meat for many days.

As we descended further, the mountain mist began to lift to reveal a wonderful sight.

There, some five thousand feet or so below, stretched mile after mile of greenery. The landscape lay before us like a map, patches of forest here, rich undulating grassland there, broken by a glistening blue river. In the distance, we could just make out roaming herds of game or cattle, and groups of dome-shaped huts.

"Look!" cried Sir Henry, pointing at a wide, white path to our right that led from the mountain and sliced its way through the countryside. "Remember Silvestre's map – that must be Solomon's Road!"

Chapter 5

Kingdom of the Kukuanas

We followed the curious man-made path as it snaked its way down the mountainside to the valley below.

It wasn't long before we left the mountain altogether and continued our journey through a wooded landscape, through which a brook babbled along merrily. The whole place was like paradise on Earth.

We decided to stop to take a much needed bath, and were engrossed in our preparations, when a flash of light whizzed past Good's head.

Turning, I saw a group of tall, copper-skinned men, dressed in leopard skin cloaks and plumes of white feathers. At their head was a muscular boy of seventeen or so.

He was crouched in the pose of a warrior who has just unleashed a weapon. Sure enough, embedded in a tree, a few feet from us, was a large knife.

The youth lunged toward us, but was held in check by an elderly warrior.

"I am Infadoos," declared this man, in a tongue so similar to Zulu it was simple to understand. "And this is Scragga," he said, pointing at the scowling boy, "son of King Twala – Twala the one-eyed, the wicked, the terrible."

"Like father, like son," complained Good, though under his breath.

"Where have you come from?" demanded Infadoos. "And what are you?" he added, clearly mystified by the pale skin of most of our party.

"We come in peace from beyond the mountains," I replied.

"You lie," said Scragga. "No man can cross the mountains where all things perish. But whoever you are, no strangers may live in the land of the Kukuanas. It's the King's law. Prepare to die!"

As one, the men surrounded us and raised the fearsome-looking spears they were carrying.

"Wait!" I cried, gesturing to Umbopa to hand me one of the rifles. "We come from another world, from the biggest star that shines at night. I'll prove it to you."

I pointed to an antelope grazing about seventy yards away. "Can an ordinary man bring down a beast from here with just a noise?" I asked.

"It isn't possible," replied Infadoos.

I took aim, fired, and, accompanied by a loud crack from my weapon, the antelope fell to earth. A gasp arose from the Kukuanas.

"These are wizards indeed," said the elderly warrior, who had clearly never seen any type of firearm before. "They must meet the King."

"Lead us then, to Twala," I cried.

"And also, let us hope, to my brother," added Sir Henry.

Chapter 7
Twala the Terrible

As we made the journey along the white road, Infadoos told me more of his king.

Apparently, Twala had killed his twin brother Imotu many years ago in order to seize the throne. Imotu's wife had then fled to the mountains with her infant son, Ignosi, and both were presumed dead.

"If he were still alive, Ignosi would be the rightful ruler of the Kukuanas," declared Infadoos with some feeling. I got the impression that he didn't much care for Twala.

After two days, we arrived at Leu, the main settlement of Kukuanaland, which lay at the foot of a large hill. Fifty miles or so in the distance, three snow-capped mountains towered over the hundreds of dwellings.

"It is said that those mountains once brought wise men of old to our country," said Infadoos. "Now our kings are buried there, in the Place of Death."

"That must be the site of King Solomon's Mines," I whispered to Sir Henry and the others, recalling the map.

We were led into the heart of the settlement and made comfortable in a large hut. After we had eaten, Umbopa inquired about Sir Henry's brother, but sadly met with no success.

"Perhaps he never got here?" suggested Good. "We only discovered it by a miracle."

"I don't know," said Sir Henry thoughtfully. "But somehow I'm sure I'll find him."

Presently, Infadoos returned to say that Twala was ready to meet us. We followed him to the heart of the settlement and were seated before a massive hut. Around it stood thousands of warriors, each one as still as a statue.

The hut door opened, and a gigantic cloaked figure emerged. His cruel-looking face was made even more terrifying by the fact that he had just one gleaming black eye.

This giant was joined by Scragga, and what at first appeared to be a withered-up monkey, wrapped in a fur cape.

"Be humble, oh people," piped this creature in a thin voice. "It is the King."

"It is the King," boomed out the thousands of warriors in answer.

Silence followed, broken only by the clatter of a spear falling to the ground.

Twala cast his single eye in the direction of the warrior who had dropped his weapon.

"Would you make your King look foolish in front of these strangers from the stars?" he snapped.

The King nodded to Scragga, who gave an ugly grin. The next second, a spear flew from the youth's hand and went hurtling clean through the unfortunate soldier.

I could see that Sir Henry was boiling with rage at what had just happened.

"Keep quiet, for heaven's sake," I whispered to him. "Our lives depend on it."

Twala turned to us. "Should I do the same to you?" he asked, threateningly.

"Touch one hair of our heads and destruction

shall come upon you," I said, as firmly as I could under the circumstances.

Taking up my rifle, I fired a shot at the spear, causing the blade to shatter.

At this, the monkey-like attendant threw off its cloak to reveal a body that resembled a withered, sun-dried corpse. She placed a skinny claw on Twala's shoulder and fixed her beady black eyes on us.

"What seek you, white men of the stars?" she croaked. "Do you seek a lost one... or bright stones? You shall not find them here."

Then she turned her bald vulture-head towards Umbopa. "And what do you seek?" she sneered. "Ha! I think I know."

She raised her skeletal arms skyward. "Blood, blood, blood!" she screeched. "There will be rivers of blood, I foretell it!"

219

Chapter 6

Umbopa's Secret

We returned to our hut, and after a brief discussion with Sir Henry and Good, I shared our thoughts with Infadoos.

"We feel that Twala is a cruel king," I said.

"It's true, my lords," sighed the old warrior. "The land cries out with his cruelties. The innocent die, just for his pleasure. And if Twala fears a man, he will make that wizened witch, Gagool, smell that man out as a wizard, and he will be killed."

"Why do your people not rise up against him?" asked Sir Henry.

"Then Scragga would reign in his place," replied Infadoos, "and the heart of Scragga is blacker than the heart of Twala. If only Ignosi had lived..."

"I did," said Umbopa.

We all looked in amazement at the man.

"I am Ignosi, rightful King of the Kukuanas," he declared proudly.

"How can that be?" asked Infadoos.

"After my father Imotu was killed by Twala, my mother and I joined a wandering tribe, till at length she died. I carried on alone, until I reached the north and lived among the white men. But I always knew I would return to my own people one day."

"So that's why you joined our expedition," said Good.

Infadoos was not yet convinced. "If you are truly the son of Imotu, you will bear the mark of the great snake," he said.

With that, Umbopa lifted his shirt to reveal a magnificent deep blue tattoo of a snake, coiled dramatically around his waist.

Infadoos fell upon his knees. "It's the King!"

"Rise," said Umbopa. "I am not yet King, but with your help and that of these brave white men, I shall be."

We began to make plans. There was to be a great dance for our benefit tomorrow. Infadoos would use this distraction to round up the local chiefs on the nearby hill and persuade them to join Umbopa's cause. We were to join him there after the dancing.

The next afternoon, we were brought before Twala once more. This time, the warriors had been replaced by beautiful girls.

"Let the dance begin," cried Twala.

At this, the girls began whirling around and around, singing a sweet song.

One by one, they pirouetted in front of us with the grace of the greatest ballet dancers.

"Which is the prettiest, white men?" asked Twala as the dancing ended.

"The first," I replied, without thinking.

"Then she must die!" announced Twala. "Scragga, make sharp your spear."

Umbopa strode up to Twala defiantly. "I will kill you before you kill this girl."

Twala looked shocked. "Who are you to challenge Twala the Terrible?"

Umbopa's chest swelled with pride. "I am Ignosi, true King of the Kukuanas!"

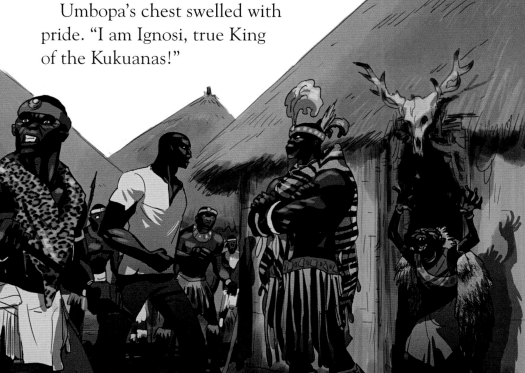

Undaunted, Scragga raised his weapon.

"Stop!" cried Sir Henry, rushing forward to the bloodthirsty youth.

Animated by fear or fury, Scragga drove his spear with all his force at Sir Henry's broad chest.

With an agility for which I would not have given him credit, Sir Henry dodged the blow with only a whisker to spare.

Before Scragga had time to strike again, Sir Henry snatched up the spear and sent it straight through his attacker.

At this, the dancing girls ran off in all directions, screeching in panic, and we took the opportunity to make good our escape.

Chapter 8
The battle for Kukuanaland

When we reached the hill, we found Infadoos had not been idle. Thousands of warriors were converging on the summit.

The chiefs were called for and Umbopa, or rather Ignosi, told his story once more. Soon they bowed down before him, just as Infadoos had done.

"Now," announced Infadoos, "we must prepare to fight."

It became clear that Twala's forces had the same idea. From our vantage point we could make out small groups scuttling to and fro from the main settlement in search of reinforcements.

"They won't attack until darkness has passed," said Ignosi. "We must make ready."

As dawn approached, Ignosi gave us our orders. Sir Henry, along with Infadoos and his regiment of old warriors known as the Greys, would attack the front of Twala's column. A group led by Ignosi and myself would then back them up. Meanwhile, Good would join the attack on Twala's right flank, and another group would engage the left.

We had brought our rifles with us, but scarcity of ammunition, coupled with the sheer numbers of troops amassed against us, meant they were next to useless. So we armed ourselves with spears, fearsome looking knives and hide-covered iron shields.

As we went to our posts, we wished each other luck, though I doubted whether any of us would live to see the sunset.

Taking my position with Ignosi, I watched anxiously as Twala's troops stormed out of the settlement, and the Greys surged down the hillside to confront them.

Soon the two sides became entangled amid the clashing of shields, spears and knives.

For what seemed an eternity, the battle raged on, until it became clear that the Greys had the upper hand. They overran their opponents and took up a defensive position on a raised knoll, halfway between our hill and the main settlement.

Then Ignosi raised his spear above his head, gave the piercing Kukuana battle cry and we charged down the hill to join our allies.

I can recall little of what happened next, save that I seemed to get caught up in a sea of warriors.

The next thing I knew, I found myself deposited, battered and bruised, at Sir Henry's feet atop the knoll. But my relief at finding my friend alive was tempered by the sight of Twala's men determinedly surging forward.

Again and again, they attacked. Again and again, we beat them back.

Suddenly, Twala himself emerged from the ranks and lashed out at Sir Henry with his vicious blade, catching him a fearful blow on the face. Blood poured from the wound.

My friend staggered back, and I feared he was done for, as Twala threw himself at Sir Henry in a fresh assault.

Sir Henry's mighty hand gripped Twala's muscular arm to prevent him landing a fatal blow. Somehow the weapon was wrested from the King's grasp, and the next second Sir Henry swung it around his head, before hitting his opponent with all his force. There was a shriek of horror from a thousand throats, as Twala's head sprang from his shoulders and fell at Ignosi's feet.

At that moment, a deafening battle cry filled the air, and the two remaining regiments, with Captain Good somewhere among them, swarmed down to trap our enemy in a pincer movement.

The opposing forces engaged, but Twala's men had lost the will to put up a struggle. In just five minutes, the fate of the battle was decided. My friends and I stood in silence, exhausted.

Around us, the dead and the dying lay in piled-up masses. It had come at a terrible price, but the reign of Twala the Terrible was at an end.

Chapter 9

King Solomon's Mines

It was several days before any of us were fit enough to turn our attention to the original objective of our expedition.

Sir Henry still believed there was a chance that his brother had made it to the mines.

He had no interest in their content however, agreeing that Good and I should divide any spoils between us. I rather felt that a share of the fabled diamonds would be just compensation for what we'd all been through.

Now formally crowned king, Ignosi ordered Gagool to guide us to The Three Witches. This was the local name for the imposing triangle of mountains which we'd seen on our arrival.

So it was that, early one morning, and with
ill-concealed hostility, Gagool led Sir Henry, Good,
Infadoos and myself along the final stretch of the
great white road.

Three days later, we reached the foot of the
mountains, where we came upon the first of many
breathtaking sights. Before us was a massive hole in
the earth, some three hundred feet deep and about
half a mile across.

"This must be the mine," I exclaimed in awe.
All around the rim I could see areas that had
been levelled out, in order to remove the stones.
But, search as we might, there was no sign of the
legendary gemstones themselves.

We marched on, and circled the pit until we rejoined the road. It was early evening when we first made out three towering shapes at the foot of the mountains. As we got nearer, I realized that they were magnificent statues, carved out of the rock.

"Behold the Silent Ones," said Infadoos reverently.

"I think they must be ancient gods, conceived by some Phoenician architect, I shouldn't wonder," suggested Sir Henry.

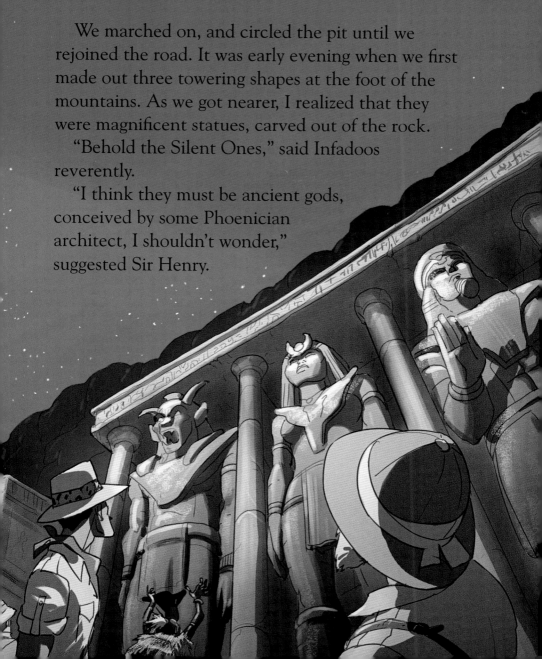

Passing by the statues, Gagool led us to an arched portal in the rockface.

"Now, white men from the stars," she said with a wicked grin, "are you ready? I must obey my king and show you the store of bright stones."

Sir Henry, Good and I nodded. But as we made to go inside, Infadoos hung back.

"It's not for me to enter there," he said with a frown, clearly bound by some age-old law. "But be warned, Gagool. If harm comes to my lords, you shall die."

Our way lit by a gourd of oil carried by the old witch, we walked along the narrow passage until at last we emerged into a vast, cathedral-like cave.

The place must have been a hundred feet high, dimly lit from above somehow, and was lined with shining white stalactites that resembled giant pillars of ice. I could have spent many hours examining this wondrous sight, but Gagool was eager to get her business over.

She led us to the top of the cave, through a doorway and along another passage which emerged into a much smaller chamber.

As Gagool's evil chuckle echoed around us, I stood transfixed by its grisly contents. They will remain engraved on my mind until the day I die.

Chapter 10
The Place of Death

Towering over the room was a massive human skeleton. It was carved out of white stalactite, which gave it an eerie luminescence. In its hand was a spear.

But this bizarre spectacle was not the worst of it. Seated on a low stone table was the body of King Twala, his head resting upon his knees.

Water dripped down onto his body from the ceiling. Its intended effect was clear. For, seated around the table, were what at first appeared to be smaller versions of the stalactites we'd seen in the cave.

On closer inspection, we realized that they were mummified bodies, encased to a greater or lesser degree, by rock formed by the trickling water.

"You know who they are, of course?" whispered Good after a time.

"The former rulers of Kukuanaland, I fear," replied Sir Henry. "Petrified, one and all."

"What a ghastly way to bury the dead," said Good.

"Now Gagool," I said in a low voice, "lead us to the treasure chamber."

Gagool hobbled into the shadows to a featureless wall behind the skeleton. "Here is the chamber, my lords."

"Don't jest with us," I said sternly, surveying the flat, solid rock.

"I do not jest," she cried. "See!"

At that instant, a mass of stone slowly rose from the floor and disappeared into the rock above.

I guessed that Gagool had operated some secret lever, though she had been careful to avoid us seeing anything at all.

We made our way down a dim tunnel, at the end of which stood an elaborately carved wooden doorway. At last we stood on the threshold of the treasure room.

"Enter my lords," rasped Gagool. "But be warned, there is a saying that those who enter there will die within a moon!"

"Oh confound it all," said Good, grabbing Gagool's lamp and shoving open the door. "I'm not going to be frightened by her."

"Let my lords look for a nook," said Gagool, as we entered the small room. "In the nook you will find what you seek."

After a certain amount of fumbling around in the dark, we located a recess in the wall. Within it sat three stone chests. The lid of one had been removed and lay resting by its side. Sir Henry held the lamp over it.

"Look!" he gasped.

The chest was piled high with dazzling, uncut diamonds, most of them a considerable size. An examination of the other chests revealed the same.

I stooped and picked up a generous handful of the stones. "We're the richest men in the whole world," I gasped.

For a minute or so, we stood transfixed by the wealth before us. But our moment of triumph was short lived.

"Hee, hee! Farewell, foolish men from the stars!" came a cry from outside the room.

We ran from the treasure room to find Gagool standing on our side of the stone door, which was rapidly descending. With a last cackle, she ducked through the decreasing gap leading back to the Place of Death.

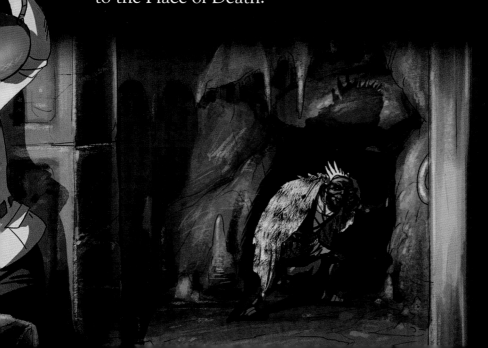

But Gagool had left her escape too late. The thirty ton slab caught her in its vice-like grip, until her body was pressed flat against the rock floor. There was a blood-curdling shriek, followed by a long, sickening crunch. Gagool the witch was no more.

"Good riddance," I said, unable to feel any pity for such a wicked creature.

"We may soon join her," sighed Sir Henry.

"Eh? What do you mean?" asked Good.

"Don't you see, man?" said Sir Henry gravely. "We're trapped."

Chapter 11
Buried alive

We spent the next hour frantically searching the passageway for a device that might release the door, but to no avail. We concluded that the control must be in the Place of Death. Gagool had operated it, then ducked back into the passageway for a last gloat. This risky act had cost her her life.

Very soon, the oil in the gourd ran out and we found ourselves in total darkness, which only added to the horror of our situation.

We had a small supply of matches, but decided to use them sparingly.

I wondered how long it would take before Infadoos would dare to come after us. Days perhaps? But even if he did, would he ever find the secret entrance to our tomb?

Only by our watches could we judge that night had turned to day, and then to night once more.

In the early hours of the morning, a thought suddenly occurred to me.

"How is it that the air keeps fresh?" I asked. "That stone door is air-tight."

"Good heavens, you're right," said Good. "It must come from somewhere. Let's look."

We scrambled around the chamber, feeling for a crack in the rock. At last, Good felt a faint gust of air coming through the floor. He rose and stamped on the place. It rang hollow.

I rubbed my hands over the ground and felt a stone ring, set level with the rock. Heaving with our combined force, we raised the flagstone until, with a rush of air, it fell aside. I lit a match and peered into the hole. I could hardly believe our luck. There were the first steps of a stone staircase.

As we prepared to leave, I couldn't resist pausing to fill every available pocket with diamonds from one of the chests.

"Won't you fellows take some with you?" I asked, as Good vanished from view.

"Oh, hang the diamonds!" said Sir Henry. "I hope I never see another."

And so we descended.

I counted fifteen steps, which ended in a labyrinth of tunnels. We spent the next few hours groping our way along, most of the time in darkness, hoping that the ground beneath our feet wouldn't give way without warning.

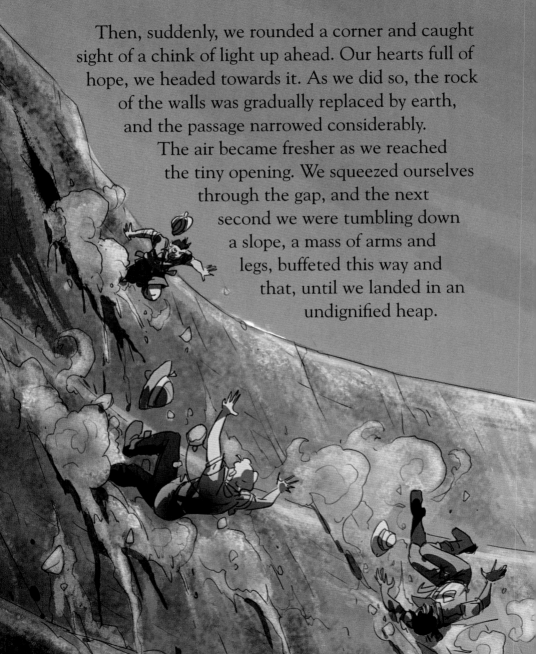

Then, suddenly, we rounded a corner and caught sight of a chink of light up ahead. Our hearts full of hope, we headed towards it. As we did so, the rock of the walls was gradually replaced by earth, and the passage narrowed considerably. The air became fresher as we reached the tiny opening. We squeezed ourselves through the gap, and the next second we were tumbling down a slope, a mass of arms and legs, buffeted this way and that, until we landed in an undignified heap.

Feeling somewhat battered and bruised, we struggled to our feet and took in our surroundings.

"It's the pit!" cried Sir Henry.

Sure enough, we had emerged at the bottom of the mine workings we had seen on our arrival at The Three Witches. It seemed a lifetime ago.

Somehow, we found the strength to scale the side of the crater, until at last we reached ground level once more.

As we did so, a familiar figure rushed along the road towards us.

"Oh my lords!" shouted Infadoos. "It is indeed you, come back from the dead!"

The old warrior flung himself at our feet and wept with joy.

Chapter 12
A final surprise

W hen we returned to Leu, Ignosi made many generous offers to us to stay, but we were all eager to get home. My only regret was that we had not been successful in our original objective. I could see the sadness in Sir Henry's eyes as we left the settlement, surrounded as we were by hundreds of cheering Kukuanas.

Infadoos told us of another route to the desert, just north of Sheba's Peaks, which was considerably quicker and less hazardous than the one we had taken. The old warrior came with us as far as he could, then bade us a tearful farewell.

Three days later, we had left that wonderful hidden land behind us and were well across the desert. It was then that something quite extraordinary occurred.

As we approached an oasis to fill our water bottles, a curious sight met our eyes. Not twenty yards ahead was a small hut.

At that moment a tanned man, with a big black beard and clad in skins, emerged from the hut. He seemed to be lame, and as he hobbled towards us, he gave a cry. When he got closer, he exchanged looks with Sir Henry and then collapsed in a sort of faint.

"Great powers!" gasped Sir Henry. "It's... It's my brother, George!"

Presently George recovered, and he and his brother hugged each other with joy. Whatever they had argued about in the past, it was evidently forgotten now.

We were joined by Jim, the guide to whom I had given directions to the mines all those years ago. He told us how he'd lost the note, and that he and Sir Henry's brother had taken an alternate route.

It was while resting at this oasis that George had met with an accident, when a boulder became dislodged and landed on his leg.

Unable to walk any distance, he'd remained here with his faithful servant ever since. The oasis had provided their water, and the animals that frequented it, their food.

That night we joined George and Jim around a campfire and recounted our own adventures.

"By Jove, Henry," said George, when we had shown him the diamonds, "at least you have got something to show for your pains, besides my worthless self."

"They belong to Quatermain and Good," laughed Sir Henry. "It was part of the bargain that they should share any spoils."

Good and I later tried to persuade Sir Henry to take a third share, but he'd have none of it. So, with his consent, we agreed to give them to his brother, who'd suffered as much as we had in the search for the treasure.

Our journey back to Sitanda's Kraal was an arduous one, especially as we had to support George. But somehow we managed it.

Five months later, Sir Henry, George and Captain Good set sail for England, while I returned to my little house in Durban.

Not long ago, I received a letter from Sir Henry, inviting me to stay with him in England for a time, if only to write an account of our amazing adventures.

And do you know, I think I'll take him up on his offer. Somehow it's a task I don't like to entrust to anybody else.

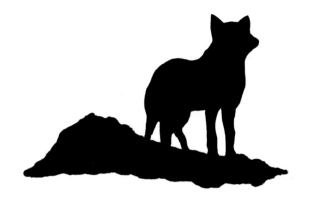

White Fang

In Jack London's novel, half-dog and half-wolf White Fang begins his journey in the Yukon, a remote area of north west Canada. In 1896, gold was discovered there in a tributary of the Klondike River, quickly named Bonanza Creek. Over 30,000 people rushed to the territory to see if they could make their fortunes.

Chapter 1
The cub

While his eyes were still closed, the little cub knew his mother, who gave him food, warmth and love. Deep inside the cave, he snuggled close to her and dozed.

When his eyes opened, the first thing he saw was the light at the mouth of the cave. It drew him to it. He was always crawling and sprawling towards the edge of the cave, and his mother was always nudging him back with her nose.

One day, when his mother was out hunting, he crawled right up to the dazzling wall of light.

He crept to the edge of the cave and looked out and saw the world. It was so bright, he was terrified and he crouched down. He gazed around, until he forgot he was scared, and he stepped out boldly into the air...

...and yelped loudly as he rolled all the way to the bottom of a long bumpy slope.

White Fang

When he finally came to a stop, he sat up. He licked the mud off himself and looked around, as might the first man from Earth when he landed on the unknown Mars.

He began to move, clumsily, running into twigs, falling over logs and stubbing his toes and nose on rocks and branches. Before long, he tripped and fell into a bird's nest.

There were seven chicks in it, and at first the cub was scared of them. But they smelled good. He picked one up and put it in his mouth. It was delicious meat, and he didn't stop until he had eaten all seven.

He was just licking his lips when a feathered whirlwind bowled him over. It was the furious mother of the chicks, who pecked and pecked at him until he turned and fled.

The cub ran and ran, until he came to a clearing and lay down. He was tired. Suddenly, more than anything in the world, he wished for his mother. So he started to look for the cave, feeling lonely and helpless and lost.

He had stumbled a few paces when a strange creature with flashing yellow eyes appeared: a weasel!

With a cry, the weasel rushed at him. He felt teeth sink into his throat. Snarling, the cub scrambled back, but the weasel held on and the snarl became a whimper.

The little cub would have died but, at that moment, his mother came bounding up.

The weasel let go of the cub and leaped at the she-wolf. With one flick of her head, the she-wolf flung the weasel into the air and caught it in her snapping jaws.

She nuzzled her cub and licked his cuts, as happy to find him as he was to be found. After eating the weasel together, they trotted home to their cave.

Soon after that, the cub began to go out hunting with his mother. He knew the law now: eat or be eaten. So he ate creatures that flew into the air, or ran away, or faced and fought him. Running and hunting made him happy. And, after he hunted, he lazed in the sunshine with a full belly. He was alive, excited and very proud of himself.

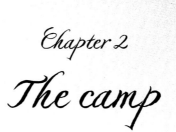

Chapter 2

The camp

One day, as he was trotting through the forest, the cub saw and smelled five live things that he had never seen before. He wanted to run away, but he was so scared he froze.

Five men sat around a fire, although the cub didn't know they *were* men – or what fire was. One of them stooped over him, and the cub bristled, baring his little fangs.

"Look! The white fangs!" the man said, laughing. He reached down to pick up the cub, and the cub bit his hand.

The next moment, the cub was knocked over by a sharp blow. He sat up and cried loudly. He waited for his brave mother to dash in and save him.

His mother did come bounding up, snarling
fiercely, but the cub was astonished by what
happened next.

"Kiche!" one of the men cried out in surprise.
"It's Kiche!"

The little cub saw his proud mother sink to the
ground, whimpering and wagging her tail.

"It's been a year since she ran away, Gray Beaver,"
a man said, slipping a tether around her neck.

Gray Beaver nodded. "Her father was dog, and

her mother was wolf," he replied. "But this little cub is nearly all wolf. His fangs are white, so White Fang will be his name. He will be my dog. I have spoken."

So the cub had a new home – the camp in the forest. He didn't like it. His mother was tied to a stick all day, and there were other dogs at the camp that rushed at him and scared him.

Still, he was amazed by the powerful men and their strange, colossal teepees, and by every new thing he discovered.

One day, he watched Gray Beaver rubbing two sticks together.

Something bright rose from the sticks, twisting and turning. White Fang crawled towards the flame and slowly put out his tongue.

He jumped back, and burst out in an explosion of howls and cries. The pain hurt more than anything he had ever known. While he cried and cried, the men burst out laughing.

White Fang understood that the men were laughing at him, and the laughter hurt him most of all. So he fled to his mother, the one creature in the world who was not laughing at him.

White Fang's mother was always there to protect him. But there was one thing she could not save him from: Lip-lip.

Lip-lip was a puppy like White Fang, but he was older, and he was a bully. He picked on White Fang whenever he strayed from his mother's side.

White Fang had no friends – Lip-lip made sure of that. He never played like a puppy – Lip-lip would not allow it. Soon, he got all the dogs to attack White Fang.

So White Fang became crafty, swift and cruel. He became as agile as a cat. He learned to fight all the dogs at once – he had to, or he would not have survived.

Then, one dreadful day, his mother was taken away, down the river in a canoe.

That night, White Fang howled and howled. He howled so much that Gray Beaver woke up and hit him.

When he was old enough,
White Fang started to pull a sled
with seven other dogs. He was the
leader of the team – and this made the
other dogs hate him even more.

All the other dogs saw all day was his waving
brush of a tail and his hind legs fleeing away, and it
made them long to attack him.

White Fang

Each night, when they were out of the harness, they sprang on him. White Fang had to fight them off with vicious snarls and bites.

"There's never been another one like White Fang," Gray Beaver said. "Never one so hated by his own kind, or so strong. I prize him more every day."

Chapter 3
Beauty

That summer, Gray Beaver took White Fang on a journey. It was the summer of 1898, and thousands of gold hunters were going up the Yukon river to try their luck. Gray Beaver stayed in Fort Yukon, selling bales of furs and mittens to the gold hunters. He made a fortune overnight.

Soon White Fang saw his first white men. They were strange looking, but their dogs didn't amount to much. The dogs were afraid of him. They could sense that White Fang was from the wild.

White Fang and a gang of other dogs enjoyed wreaking havoc among the white men's dogs, and the men in Fort Yukon enjoyed watching. One man always watched White Fang and cheered him on. He was called Beauty by the other men, although he was anything but a beauty. He had dirty yellow eyes, dirty yellow teeth and dirty yellow hair, and he was known as the greatest coward in the country.

"How much for your dog?" Beauty Smith asked Gray Beaver.

"I won't sell him, not for any price," Gray Beaver replied. "He's the strongest sled dog I have."

But the next week, Beauty Smith came back with a black bottle of whisky for Gray Beaver.

Every week or so he brought another bottle. Before long, Gray Beaver wanted more and more whisky and his money began to run out. The shorter his money was, the shorter his temper. The next time Beauty visited him, his goods, his money and his temper were all gone.

"I could pay you for that dog in whisky," Beauty said, his lip curling with excitement.

"You catch the wolf, you can keep him," Gray Beaver replied.

"I'll bring the bottle, you catch him," Beauty said.

The next time White Fang came back to camp, Gray Beaver slung a noose around his neck and handed the end to Beauty Smith. White Fang's hair rose on end. He bared his teeth. He could sense that Beauty was cruel.

As Beauty started to lead him away, White Fang hurled himself at him, but Beauty was ready and knocked White Fang to the ground.

White Fang crawled limply to his feet, and followed Beauty Smith, his tail between his legs.

At home, Beauty tied him up and went to bed.

Once Beauty was asleep, White Fang bit through the rope in seconds, and trotted happily back to his master.

The next day, Gray Beaver took him straight back to Beauty, and White Fang got a terrible beating. That night, he ran home to Gray Beaver again.

When Gray Beaver handed him over for the third time, Beauty beat him to within an inch of his life. At first he couldn't stand up, and Beauty had to wait for an hour before they could head off. Sick, blind and reeling, White Fang followed Beauty. This time, he was tied with a chain.

Chapter 4
The fighting wolf

Beauty Smith kept White Fang in a small pen. He loved to tease and torture him. He soon discovered that White Fang hated being laughed at and so he laughed at him all the time.

In that pen, White Fang became more savage than ever. He hated the chain that bound him, the men that laughed at him, and the dogs that came and snarled at him. Most of all, he hated Beauty Smith.

White Fang

There was a reason why Beauty Smith was making White Fang so angry. One day, he brought a crowd of men to the pen. Beauty entered, club in hand, and slipped the chain from White Fang's neck.

Then a huge dog – a mastiff – was thrust into the pen. White Fang had never seen a dog like it. But now, at last, he could unleash all his hatred. He leaped in with a flash of fangs that ripped the dog's neck. The dog plunged at White Fang, but White Fang was here, there and everywhere, jumping up and escaping him.

"Come on White Fang!" Beauty roared.

In the end, the mastiff was dragged out by its owner. White Fang had won. The men paid their bets to each other, and coins clinked in Beauty Smith's hand.

Beauty Smith quickly brought more dogs to fight White Fang. He never lost his footing, and he had a lightning quickness.

He won every fight, and every fight was a fight to the death. Before long, White Fang was known far and wide as the *Fighting Wolf*.

That autumn, Beauty Smith took White Fang north on the steamboat, and people paid money to look at him and poke sticks at him through the bars of his cage.

When he wasn't being prodded and stared at, White Fang fought. He fought dogs, wolves and, once, a full grown lynx. Then there were no more animals strong enough to fight him, until a man came to town with a bulldog. For a week, the promised fight was the talk of the town.

Chapter 5
To the death

Beauty Smith slipped the chain from White Fang's neck and stepped back.

For once, White Fang did not attack. He stood still, his ears pricked up.

"Come on, Cherokee," someone shouted.

"Come on, White Fang!" Beauty yelled.

The bulldog's owner pushed him into the ring, and he growled.

White Fang's hair stood up on end. He had never seen a dog like this. But with a catlike swiftness he slashed with his fangs at the bulldog's ear.

Cherokee followed after White Fang, but White Fang sprang in again, slashed again, and got away untouched.

Still, his strange enemy only followed him slowly around the ring.

White Fang danced and dodged, leaping in and out, biting the bulldog.

The bulldog just followed him slowly. Sooner or later he would get his teeth around White Fang's neck, and then he would win the battle.

"Do it Cherokee!" the men shouted. "Come on Cherokee!"

White Fang

White Fang rushed again at Cherokee. This time he hit him so hard, the momentum threw White Fang into the air. For the first time in his fighting life he lost his footing. He fell onto his side – and Cherokee's teeth closed on his throat.

White Fang sprang to his feet and tore wildly around, trying to shake off the bulldog. Around and around he went, barking madly and trying to shake off the great weight. But Cherokee shut his eyes and held on.

The bulldog was slowly throttling White Fang. He fell to his side and lay still, panting for breath. It looked as if the battle was over.

Then Beauty Smith began to laugh, and White Fang went wild with rage. He got to his feet and stumbled madly around. But Cherokee still held on.

"Cherokee! Cherokee!" shouted the crowd, and Cherokee thumped his tail.

When Beauty saw White Fang's eyes begin to
close, something snapped inside him. He jumped
into the ring, and began to kick him savagely. Just
then, a stranger jumped out of the crowd.

"You coward! You beast!" he shouted, landing
Beauty with a punch. Beauty Smith lurched at him,
so he punched him again, and Beauty fell back.

"Come on Matt, lend a hand," he called to his friend, and the two men jumped into the ring to help White Fang.

They tried to loosen the dogs, but the bulldog's jaws were locked on White Fang's throat.

"Beasts!" he said to the onlookers. "Won't at least some of you help?"

But the crowd only cheered him sarcastically. Still, he got his revolver between the jaws of the bulldog, and slowly pried them apart. Very slowly, he managed to pull White Fang's mangled neck free.

As Cherokee was dragged away, White Fang sank down into the snow. His eyes were half closed, and he looked as if he had been strangled to death.

"He's just about all in," Matt said, "but he's breathin' all right."

Beauty Smith was on his feet again.

"Say, how much is a dog worth, all mangled like that?" the stranger asked.

"About a hundred and fifty dollars," someone called out.

"Then that's what I'm going to give you for him," the stranger told Beauty.

Beauty Smith put his hands behind his back. "I ain't a-selling," he said.

"Oh yes you are," the man replied. "Because I'm buying. Here's your money. The dog's mine."

"I'm a man, I've got my rights."

"You're not a man, you're a beast," the man spat at Beauty. "Do you want the money, or do I have to hit you again?"

"I'll have the law on you," Beauty said.

"If you open your mouth, I'll hound you out of town. Understand?"

"Yes," Beauty muttered.

"Yes what?"

"Yes, sir," Beauty snarled.

"Who *is* he?" a man in the crowd whispered.

"Weedon Scott," someone answered. "A mining expert. He's in with all the big wigs. If you want to keep out of trouble, you'll steer clear of him."

So Beauty Smith stumbled away, cursing to himself, and Weedon Scott took White Fang home.

Chapter 6
A new life

"It's hopeless," Weedon confessed. He and Matt were looking out of their cabin at White Fang. Matt shrugged. Together they watched White Fang on the end of his tether, snarling and bristling.

"He's a wolf and there's no taming him," Weedon said. "We've had him two weeks, and he's wilder than he's ever been. What can I do?"

"Turn him loose," Matt advised, "and take a club with you."

So Weedon went over to White Fang, and loosed the rope from around his neck. White Fang could hardly believe it. Since he had belonged to Beauty, he had not known a single moment of freedom.

"There, there," Weedon said soothingly, "I'm not gonna hurt you."

But White Fang was suspicious. Something was going to happen. He bristled and showed his teeth. The man's hand came out and touched his head.

White Fang snarled menacingly and sank low to the ground. But the hand stayed on his head. White Fang sprang up.

"Argh!" Weedon clutched his torn, bloody hand.

White Fang crouched down and backed away. He knew now he'd get a beating as bad as any from Beauty Smith.

"What are you doing?" Scott shouted.

292

Matt had dashed into the cabin and returned with a rifle.

"I reckon I should kill 'im," said Matt.

White Fang had jumped up and was now snarling with blood-curdling viciousness at Matt. The two men stared at him. Wherever the rifle pointed, White Fang leaped away from it.

"Well look at that," Matt said. "That dog is just too intelligent to shoot."

White Fang waited for his punishment: he knew it was coming now. With his hand bandaged, Weedon walked up to him and sat down a short distance away. He had no club in his hand.

Weedon began to talk and the hair rose on White Fang's neck. He growled.

But Weedon talked to White Fang as he had never been talked to before – soothingly and gently. In spite of himself, White Fang began to be less afraid.

After a long time, Weedon stood up and went into the cabin. White Fang expected him to return with a gun, but he came back with a small piece of meat and tossed it onto the snow. White Fang's body was tense – ready to spring away from a blow. He pricked up his ears and looked at it suspiciously. There was no telling what cruelty lay behind the piece of meat.

White Fang sniffed it, keeping his eyes on the man. It smelled good. He swallowed it. It tasted good too.

He was thrown more and more pieces, and he ate them up. Finally the man refused to toss the meat. Instead he held it out with his hand. With his ears flattened back, White Fang growled as he crept forward, took the meat from the hand... and nothing happened.

He ate more meat, and still there was no punishment. But now the hand came down to hurt him. White Fang shrank down under the hand. He growled, snarled and bristled and flattened his ears. He was ready to spring up when the blow struck.

But the blow didn't come. A hand came down on his head, and lifted up again.

White Fang knew some punishment was coming. He longed to flee, or spring up. But, at the same time, the voice soothed him. His master talked softly, and his hand rose and fell.

Although everything in him longed to run, White Fang stayed still. It was the end of an old life for White Fang. A new, much fairer life was beginning.

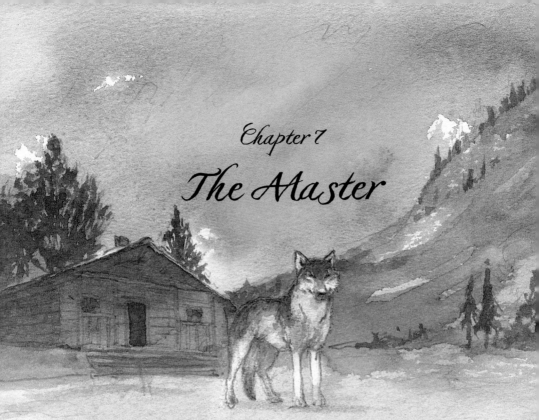

Chapter 7

The Master

Every day, Weedon patted White Fang. And, day by day, White Fang got used to being patted. At first he put up with it, but later, he even came to enjoy it.

He was too set in his ways to ever bark a welcome to his new master, or bound up to greet him. But he pulled his master's sled, and he guarded his house faithfully each night. Day by day, he grew more fond of him, although he didn't show it.

White Fang

In the spring, Weedon went away on business. A few weeks later, he received a note from Matt.

> Weedon
>
> The wolf won't work. Won't eat.
> He wants to know what has become of you,
> and I don't know how to tell him.
> Think he might die.
>
> Matt

It was true. In the cabin, White Fang lay on the floor, with no interest in food, in Matt, or in life. Matt might talk gently to him or swear at him, but it was all the same. He never did more than turn his dull eyes upon Matt, then drop his head on his forepaws.

Late one night, Matt was startled by a low whine from White Fang. He was up on his feet, his ears cocked towards the door, listening intently.

A moment later, Matt heard a footstep. The door opened, and Weedon Scott stepped in. The two men shook hands.

"Holy smoke!" Matt exclaimed. "Look at him wag his tail!"

Weedon Scott strode across the room and White Fang came to him and gazed up at him, light shining in his eyes.

"He never looked at me that way, all the time you were gone!" Matt said.

Weedon squatted down and petted White Fang. He rubbed at the roots of his ears, stroked his neck, and tapped his spine gently with the tips of his fingers.

White Fang growled affectionately, and then, quite suddenly, he nudged his way in between his master's arm and body, and snuggled there.

The two men looked at each other. Weedon's eyes were shining now.

"Gosh!" said Matt. "I always insisted that wolf was a dog. Look at him!"

White Fang was better in two days. And having learned to snuggle, he did it often.

One night, Weedon and Matt sat playing cards

when there was a loud cry and the sound of snarling outside the house. They jumped to their feet.

"The wolf's got somebody," Matt said.

"Bring a light!" Weedon shouted as he ran outside. Matt ran out after him with the lamp.

In the lamplight, they saw a man lying on his back in the snow, trying to fight off White Fang.

The next instant, Weedon had White Fang by the throat and was dragging him clear, while Matt helped the man to his feet. He gasped and let go when he saw who it was.

Beauty Smith stood blinking in the lamplight. Matt looked down and saw two objects lying in the snow, a steel dog-chain and a stout club. Matt spun Beauty around and sent him into the darkness.

"Tried to steal you, eh?" Weedon said. "And you wouldn't have it. Well, he made a mistake now, didn't he?"

"Must have thought he was fighting seventeen devils," Matt said, smirking.

That night, White Fang kept snarling, long after Beauty Smith was gone.

Chapter 8
A broken window

Something was in the air. White Fang sensed that something terrible was about to happen, even before there was any evidence for it. He lay down on the floor and gave a low, sad whine.

"That dog's on to you," Matt said. "He knows you're leaving him."

"Well, what the devil can I do with a dog in California?" Weedon replied. "He'd kill all the dogs he met on sight. The police would take him away and put him down. No, it would never do."

"You're right," Matt said. Then, after a pause, he added: "Still, there's no denying that he thinks a lot of you."

"I know my mind – and what's best!" Weedon snapped back.

The next day, White Fang spied his master packing his bags through the open cabin door. That night, he lifted his muzzle to the stars and let out a long, lonely wolf howl.

Inside the cabin, the two men were getting ready for bed.

"Listen to that, will you?" Matt said. "I wouldn't be surprised if he dies this time around."

Weedon's blankets rustled. "Oh will you be quiet and stop going on about it!"

The next day, Weedon was going to California – for good.

"Give me one last goodbye growl, won't you?" he said to White Fang. But White Fang refused.

Just then the steamship hooted on the river. The two men set off down the hill.

"Take good care of him, Matt," Weedon said.

Inside the house, White Fang had begun to howl as if his master had died.

When Weedon and Matt got to the steamship, it was jammed with people. And there, sitting on the deck, was White Fang. The two men stared at him in shock.

"You locked the doors?" Weedon asked.

"You bet I did."

"Look, there are cuts on his muzzle," Weedon said. "That crazy dog... He must have leaped clean through the window!"

"I'll take him ashore," Matt said.

The boat's whistle hooted. Weedon had to think quickly. He shook Matt's hand.

"You've no need to worry about taking care of the wolf," he said.

"What? You don't mean it?"

"I do," Weedon said.

A minute later Matt stood on the shore as the

ship set off down the river.

"He won't like the climate!" Matt shouted. "Just make sure you clip his hair in the summer!"

Weedon bent over the wolf standing beside him, patted his head and rubbed his ears. "Now growl," he said.

Chapter 9

The sleeping wolf

When the steamer arrived in San Francisco, White Fang was terrified. Cable cars hooted and clanged and screeched down the streets. There was so much noise! There were so many men! White Fang felt small, helpless and dizzy – but it was all over as quickly as a bad dream.

He was put into a carriage, and soon it was driving up to a house. When White Fang jumped out, the countryside lay all around him.

White Fang

There were lots of people to get used to at his new home. Weedon lived there with his wife, his young children and his parents.

Day by day, White Fang got used to the new people. He thought of them as precious possessions of his master, so he took great care of them.

He got used to the children petting him. And he liked sitting quietly beside Weedon's father on the porch as he read in the afternoon sun. The months came and went. White Fang grew fat, happy and content.

White Fang even grew to like Collie, the sheepdog who lived there. One afternoon, she nipped at his shoulder playfully. She ran off into the forest and he followed her. They ran together, just as his mother and father had done, years before.

Around this time, the newspapers were full of the daring escape of a murderer from prison. His name was Jim Hall, and he was on his way to get his revenge on the man who had put him behind bars: Judge Scott – Weedon's father.

White Fang

One night, while everyone was asleep, White
Fang woke up. Lying in the hall, he sniffed the air,
listened, and knew at once there was a stranger
in the house. The stranger was moving softly, but
White Fang followed silently behind him. He knew
the advantage of surprise.

The stranger paused at the foot of the staircase.
At the top of the staircase was his master and his
possessions. White Fang bristled, and waited. The
stranger lifted his foot – and White Fang struck. He
jumped through the air and landed on the stranger,
burying his fangs in his neck.

The house awoke to what sounded like a battle of devils downstairs. Shots were fired, a man screamed in horror – and the staircase was flooded with light. In the middle of the floor, a dead man was lying.

"Jim Hall," Weedon Scott said grimly.

White Fang, too, was lying on the ground. His eyes were closed.

"He's all out," Weedon muttered.

"We'll see about that," Judge Scott replied,

reaching for the telephone.

"Frankly, he has one chance in a thousand," the surgeon announced, looking down at White Fang. "Three broken ribs – one that's pierced his lungs. And three bullet holes clear through him."

"He mustn't lose any chance he has," Judge Scott said. "Spare no expense."

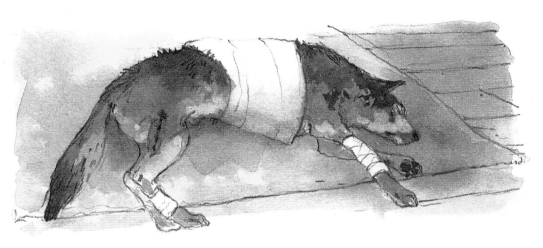

For three weeks, White Fang clung to life. He lay with his eyes closed, dreaming. He dreamed he was in the cave with his mother, or that Gray Beaver was looking down at him. Or he was back in Beauty Smith's pen, terrified. He whimpered as he dreamed of the city. At last, his bandages were taken off.

White Fang

The whole family gathered to look as White Fang rose slowly to his feet. He fell down several times, but at last he stood on his four legs.

"He'll have to learn to walk again; he might as well start now," said the surgeon.

So White Fang tottered outside. Collie lay by the stables, with six pudgy puppies playing around her in the sun.

White Fang looked on, amazed. The master shoved one little puppy towards him. He looked at the puppy, sprawled in front of him. Then their noses touched, and he licked the puppy's tiny face.

Weedon and his family clapped, but White Fang was puzzled.

White Fang

He lay down and all the puppies came to him. He let them clamber and scramble and tumble over him, and then he lay, with half-shut eyes, drowsing in the sun.

The Phantom of the Opera

The Phantom of the Opera isn't just a ghost story. Gaston Leroux's novel was based on the true tale of a mysterious figure roaming the halls of the Paris Opera House...

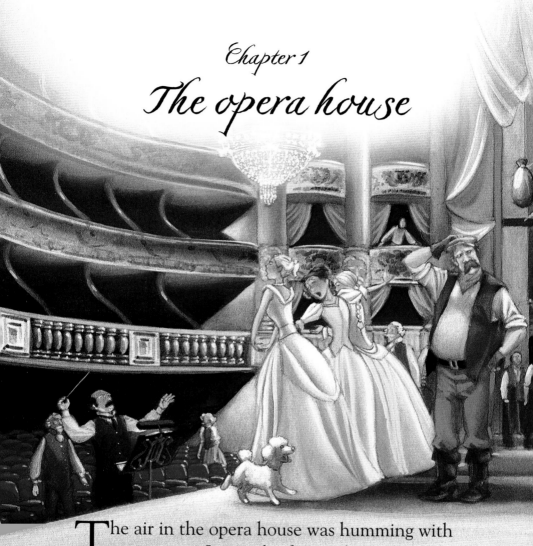

Chapter 1
The opera house

The air in the opera house was humming with excitement. It was the first night under new management. Voices were warming up with high trills and stage-hands were milling around, looking

for props. The star of the show, Carlotta, stomped around, complaining about everything.

"How can I be expected to sing," she wailed, to no one in particular, "when my throat hurts from all the smoke in this horrible city?"

Down the corridor from Carlotta, dancers fussed and fiddled with their costumes.

But in one dressing room, that evening's performance was the last thing anyone was thinking about…

"I heard the ghost has different heads that he changes as he pleases," said one of the dancers.

"I've heard he has no nose!" cried another, whose own nose was widely admired.

"You're all wrong," said a third dancer, smugly. "I've seen the phantom with my very own eyes." The others turned to stare at her.

"He has *one* head and you could mistake him for a gentleman in his long black cloak and fine hat. But I don't know about his nose, because his face was covered with a mask."

"A mask?" the girls cried.

The dancer paused dramatically.

"They say the phantom's face is SO horrific and SO frightening, it would make a grown man weep!"

"Arrgh!" screamed the girls.

"Enough of that nonsense!" interrupted Madame G, who was in charge of the show. "We have a crisis. Carlotta is refusing to sing."

The girls began to whisper among themselves.

They dragged a shy girl named Christine over to Madame G. "Christine can do it!"

"But she doesn't know the part!" cried Madame G.

"I do," said Christine softly. "I sing it every night after the show."

Madame G looked her up and down and sighed. "What choice do I have? Well, get into costume, girl. Go!"

Chapter 2

A surprising voice

The audience waited eagerly in their red velvet seats. They gazed up at the huge glass chandelier, suspended from the painted ceiling. Slowly, the lights dimmed...

The curtains went up and the cast swarmed onto the vast stage. Their voices filled the air like a chorus of angels and their bright costumes glittered as they danced.

When Christine walked on, the stage became dark and silent. A single light shone on her.

She opened her mouth and sang from her heart. It was the sweetest, most beautiful sound.

When she finished, there was silence for a moment, before loud applause erupted. The noise rang dizzily in Christine's ears and she fainted.

The audience watched in silence, as Christine's limp body was picked up and carried offstage.

She was placed in a chair in her dressing room. Madame G thrust smelling salts under her nose and she blinked open her eyes.

"My dear, you were magnificent!" said Madame G, fanning her with a handkerchief. "And you have a visitor. He's a Count!" she whispered excitedly, before rushing out.

A handsome young man came into the room. "Mademoiselle," he said, tipping his hat.

"Count, do excuse me," Christine said, trying to stand up.

"No, please rest," said the Count. "You had quite a turn."

"I just came to say," he went on, "that I'm a huge fan of the opera and I thought you were wonderful. You should sing every night!"

Christine blushed. "I... I was just standing in for Carlotta," she stammered.

"You're a million times better than her," he declared. "Anyway, I'd better go. Good night."

The Count shut the door behind him and leaned against it for a moment. He could hear a deep, male voice coming from the room.

"But there was no one else in there..." he mumbled. He had his ear to the door when a couple of dancers came by, so he quickly walked away.

Chapter 3

The phantom's demands

"What is the meaning of this?" The new manager of the opera house waved a piece of paper at Madame G.

I demand the sum of 20,000 francs per month.

P.S. Carlotta sings like a toad. I want to hear Christine sing every night or else...

P

"It's the phantom," she said nervously. "I tell the girls he isn't real. But the truth is, I've worked here for twenty years and we have always given in to him." She shuddered. "If we don't, he'll make big trouble."

"Phantom? You mean a ghost?" said the manager. "Hah! If some crook who skulks around *my* opera house thinks he can swindle money out of *me*, he's got another think coming!"

Suddenly, the door swung open and a stagehand burst in. "It's Pico! He's been taken!"

Pico was the manager's beloved pet dog.

"My little Pico! What? How? When?" spluttered the manager.

"I heard Pico barking and saw a man in a cloak in the shadows!"

Madame G shivered. "It's the phantom. Mark my words, manager. Pay up quickly or something dreadful will happen."

Chapter 4
The angel of music

The Count was hovering by Christine's dressing room. He had heard about the phantom and was worried about her, especially after hearing the strange voice in her room the week before.

"Count!" Christine almost walked into him as she came out. She looked around nervously and blocked his view into her room.

"Can I help you?" she asked, with a bright smile.

"I just wanted to make sure you were all right after fainting last week..." He paused as he heard the same deep voice coming from her room. "Who's that?"

"Oh, no one," Christine trilled. "I'm fine, thank you, but I must dash..." and she shut the door in his face.

The Count was more puzzled than ever. So he hid behind some costumes and decided to wait.

After a few minutes, Christine came out dressed in a hooded cloak. She rushed down the corridor and out of the opera house.

The Count followed her along dark, lamplit
streets, until they reached a small, gloomy graveyard.
The moonlight cast creepy shadows on the ancient
stone graves.

The Count watched as Christine knelt by a grave. The church bells began to chime midnight. Sad violin music floated on the air.

Christine swayed and sang along to the music as if in a trance. The Count was captivated...

...until he felt a hand on his shoulder that chilled him to the bone.

344

He looked into a pair of blood-red eyes and let out a scream. "Arrrrgh! The eyes, so red..." the Count spluttered.

As he spoke, the figure vanished.

"Count? What eyes? What are you talking about?" asked Christine, running over to him.

"And the violin? Did you hear the violin?" said the Count, dazed.

Christine looked afraid. "Yes, I did," she admitted, "but I don't know who's playing. I come here to sing at my father's grave. Before he died, he told me an angel of music would visit me."

"And has one?" The Count opened his eyes wide.

"He comes to the opera house," she said. "He taught me everything I know about singing – but I've never seen him."

"So the voice I heard..."

"Yes, that was him. He says I'll be the most famous singer in Paris! Will you keep it a secret?"

The Count looked serious. "If you want me to," he said. "Now let me walk you back. It's late."

Chapter 5

An unforgettable performance

The next morning was bright and sunny. Carlotta was lying in bed, eating chocolate truffles, when her maid came in with a letter.

"What's this?" Carlotta demanded,
her mouth full of chocolate.

If you appear on stage tonight,
you must be prepared for a
misfortune worse than death!
P

"It's a threat! Someone is telling me not to sing.
How dare they? Get my things, I'm going straight to
the manager."

In less than an hour, Carlotta was in the manager's office. "Monsieur!" she shrieked as she slapped down the letter.

He read it quickly and went pale. "It's the phantom," he muttered.

"Phantom?" Carlotta's ears pricked up. "I'm not afraid of a ghost. I *will* sing tonight!"

That night, the whole cast felt uneasy. But Carlotta wasn't in the least worried.

"Phantom? Pah!" she declared. She fluffed up her costume and marched on stage.

Carlotta lifted up her arms and opened her mouth
wide, but all that came out was a loud, harsh...
"Cr-r-roak!"

The audience gasped. Carlotta continued to croak
like a toad and the audience began to laugh.

The manager, who was looking on in disbelief, heard a chilling voice in his ear.

"Carlotta sings tonight to bring the house down..."
"I beg your pardon?" The manager spun around, but the figure behind him had gone.

At that moment, a deafening crack shook the hall. Everyone looked up. The glass chandelier, which sparkled above the audience, was coming loose. Plaster fell from the ceiling in great chunks and the huge light swung dangerously.

The audience began to scream and run from their seats. The singers on stage watched, horrified. With an almighty crash, the chandelier fell, narrowly missing Carlotta.

Then all of the lights went out and a terrifying, ghoulish laugh echoed around the opera house.

Chapter 6
Underground secrets

Backstage, Christine stared at the madness in terror. As she watched, a black cloak whirled around her and she was swept away.

She tried to scream for help, but her cries were muffled beneath the cloak.

Blindly, she stumbled down a flight of stairs and along a maze of twisting paths. The air around her became colder and damper as she struggled to get free.

Finally, her captor released his grip. She opened her eyes and blinked. Underneath the opera house was another world.

She saw a misty lake, with stony tunnels leading off in different directions. Huge candles flickered and wax dripped down the dark, dank walls.

"Don't be afraid, Christine," said a deep, melodic voice.

"You!" Christine gasped, spinning around. "My angel of music!"

But he wasn't what she had imagined. She came face to face with a man in a mask...

It was the Phantom of the Opera.

She took a step back, afraid.

"Don't be scared," he said. "I'm your friend. Please trust me!"

He took her shaking hand and led her onto a boat, which bobbed on the mysterious lake. The boat began to float away. Christine couldn't help but be enchanted.

"I am the voice you hear. But I'm no angel."
He turned his masked face towards the shadows.

"You are! You've been so kind to me." She paused.
"Why do you hide down here?"

"It's safe. No one can laugh at my face," the
phantom said sadly. "I'm so ugly..."

"It can't be that bad. Will you show me?"
Christine asked gently.

"No!" shouted the phantom, suddenly angry.
"Of all people I don't want to show you!"

"But you're my friend. I wouldn't turn my back
on you," she insisted.

"No Christine!" he said firmly.

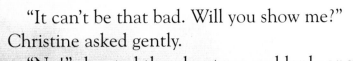

They sailed on in silence.

"Did you make the chandelier fall tonight?" she asked.

"Enough of your questions!" he roared, so loudly that Christine trembled.

"I'd better take you back," he said, a little more calmly. With one sweep of his cloak, the boat changed direction.

Chapter 7
The disappearing act

T he next day, the manager sat in his office with
Madame G.

"We must get this phantom! Little Pico is gone.
Carlotta's left us. The opera house is falling apart."

"All is not lost. Don't forget we have Christine," said Madame G.

The manager scratched his chin. "You're right. There's something magical about her... Draw up a contract. Carlotta's part is hers!"

That afternoon, posters went up all around Paris advertising the new star of the show.

Before the show, Christine nervously paced her dressing room. It was one thing to do a single performance at the last minute, quite another to be the leading lady forever.

But Christine was a born star. By the end of the show, she felt as though she had played the part all her life.

The show was almost over when the orchestra abruptly stopped playing. The chorus stopped singing and the dancers stopped dancing. The audience shifted uncomfortably in their seats.

Even the temperature seemed to drop. The only person who didn't stop was Christine. She continued to sing. With a crackle, the lights flashed and the stage went dark.

Christine let out a scream that sent shivers down everyone's spine.

The lights flared back on, lighting the stage.
A trapdoor was open and Christine had vanished.

"Christine!" shouted the Count, from his seat in
the front row.

"The phantom must have taken her," he yelled,
"through that trapdoor. Follow me!"

The manager and Madame G jumped up from
their seats and ran after the Count.

Chapter 8
The phantom's lair

The three of them disappeared under the opera house into the phantom's secret world. They ran down the twisting tunnels until they reached the lake.

"There she is!" The Count pointed to Christine who was in the boat with the phantom. Mist floated around them. "Give her back you beast! I love her!"

"No!" snarled the phantom. "She is mine now. Keep away!"

"It's for the best Count," Christine sobbed.

The phantom turned to Christine. "I only wanted to be happy, with a wife and a family."
"But you can!" Christine insisted.
"Who could love me?" he growled.

"Let her go!" shouted the Count. "Don't worry, Christine. I'm coming over!" He began to wade into the lake.

"Get back!" warned the phantom. He flicked his cloak and the water around the boat blazed into flame.

"No!" screamed Christine. "Leave him alone and I'll stay with you."

She reached up and kissed the phantom's cheek where it wasn't hidden by the mask.

Instantly, the fire went out. The phantom fell to his knees, crying.

"No one has ever kissed me. Not even my mother. You are the kindest person I have ever known."

"I told you, I'm your friend," said Christine. "But you frightened me."

"I'm so sorry," he sobbed, "I was just so lonely..."

Christine put a hand on his shoulder. They could hear police whistles in the distance.

"I must go," the phantom said.

"But..." Christine began, and paused in shock. He had vanished. All that was left in the boat was the phantom's mask. The boat floated to shore.

"Christine!" cried the Count, helping her out. "You're safe now."

They watched as the empty boat floated off into the mist.

The manager, Madame G and the police looked around in bewilderment.

Christine clutched the mask in her hands. "Goodbye, my angel of music."

About the Authors

The late nineteenth and early twentieth century was a golden age for adventure stories. More people than ever before were able to read, and books and magazines became increasingly affordable for the majority.

Authors, such as the ones in this book, were taking their readers to exciting and unusual locations, where unforgettable characters came to life and good nearly always triumphed over evil. Perhaps it's no coincidence that the lives of these authors were often as dramatic as the plots of their classic tales...

Mark Twain (1835-1910)

Mark Twain, whose real name was Samuel Langhorne Clemens, was born in Missouri, in southern USA. His life was full of adventure – journeying all over America, and working as a river pilot on the Mississippi River. When he began writing novels, he signed his work with the name Mark Twain – an expression used by river pilots to check the depth of the water. He wrote several novels, including *The Adventures of Huckleberry Finn*, which was published in 1884. By the time he died, in 1910, Twain was one of the most famous writers in America.

Robert Louis Stevenson

(1850-1894)

Robert Louis Stevenson was born in Scotland. From a young age he suffered fevers brought on by the cold Scottish weather, so he spent much of his life overseas.

His travels inspired him to write plays, poems and popular adventure stories, such as *Kidnapped* and *Treasure Island*. These made him one of the most famous writers of the 19th century. He died, aged 44, on a small island in the Pacific Ocean.

H. Rider Haggard
(1856–1925)

Henry Rider Haggard, born in Norfolk, England, was the eighth in a family of ten children. Aged nineteen, his father sent him to what is now South Africa. Back in England in 1882, he studied law, but spent most of his time writing. His stories drew on his experiences in Africa, with intrepid adventurers and lost civilizations. He wrote *King Solomon's Mines* after his brother bet him that he couldn't write a story as good as Stevenson's *Treasure Island*.

Jack London
(1876–1916)

Jack London's life was as extraordinary as his stories. Born into a poor family in San Francisco, he went to work in a factory when he was only fourteen. At fifteen, he became a pirate, stealing oysters. At seventeen, he was a sailor and at eighteen, he was sent to prison for begging. Aged twenty-one, he joined the gold rush. Six years later his first novel, *The Call of the Wild*, made him world famous. He moved to a ranch in California, USA, where he wrote many more books and short stories.

Gaston Leroux
(1868-1927)

Gaston Leroux was a French writer and journalist. He sailed the globe reporting on stories, at the same time as writing plays and novels. Today, he is best known for his novel *The Phantom of the Opera*, which first appeared serialized over several months in a French newspaper. There have been various adaptations of it since, including a silent film in 1925, and a musical in the 1980s by Andrew Lloyd Webber, which has been performed in countries all over the world.

Designed by Lenka Hrehova
Edited by Lesley Sims
Digital manipulation: Nick Wakeford

First published in 2016 by Usborne Publishing Ltd.,
83−85 Saffron Hill,London EC1N 8RT, England. www.usborne.com
Copyright © 2016, 2015, 2010, 2008 Usborne Publishing Limited.
The name Usborne and the devices ♀☿ are Trade Marks
of Usborne Publishing Ltd. All rights reserved.
First published in America in 2017. UE